Lute A. Taylor, H. A. Taylor

Lute Taylor's Chip Basket

Lute A. Taylor, H. A. Taylor

Lute Taylor's Chip Basket

ISBN/EAN: 9783744652766

Printed in Europe, USA, Canada, Australia, Japan

Cover: Foto ©Raphael Reischuk / pixelio.de

More available books at **www.hansebooks.com**

Your Friend,

Lute A. "Taylor,"

LUTE TAYLOR'S

CHIP BASKET;

BEING

CHOICE SELECTIONS

FROM THE

LECTURES, ESSAYS, ADDRESSES, EDITORIALS, AND
PUBLIC AND SOCIAL CORRESPONDENCE

OF

LUTE A. TAYLOR.

COMPILED AND EDITED BY

H. A. TAYLOR.

———————•———————

HUDSON, WIS.
STAR AND TIMES PRINTING HOUSE,
1874.

TO ALL THOSE WHO

RECOGNIZE THE GOOD, CHERISH THE TRUE,

AND

ADMIRE THE BEAUTIFUL,

THIS

LITTLE VOLUME IS RESPECTFULLY DEDICATED.

INDEX.

INTRODUCTION.

———

THE publication of this volume was not undertaken with
the expectation that it would fill any especial place in
the realm of Letters, nor that it would ever be very widely
introduced into the libraries of the general reading public.
It has been issued in compliance with a prevailing sentiment,
among the many personal friends and literary admirers of
LUTE A. TAYLOR, that his writings are worthy preservation
in permanent form, and entitled to a distinction above that
accorded to the transitory newspaper literature of the day.

With these unambitious expectations, yet confident in this
belief, the contemplated publication of this little volume was
announced. I have been alike gratified and surprised at the
general expression of satisfaction given that such a book
was to be issued, and at the great number of orders already
received for it.

In the compilation of this volume there has been no
attempt at any systematic arrangement of subjects, modi-
fication of ideas, or changes of phraseology. Although many
of the articles it contains were written in the hurry always
incident to the duties of the editor of a daily paper, and
would, no doubt, have been more polished and pungent had
the writer bestowed longer time upon them; yet we give them

mainly as found, with the occasional changes made necessary where only a portion of an article is selected.

The greatest embarrassment met with in compiling this work, has been to select from the great mass of materials before me such articles and extracts as most distinctly bear the impress of the wonderful genius, and give the clearest conception of the noble impulses and settled convictions of the writer.   -

I have gathered up but a few "chips" from among many —all hewn out by the skilled hand of a master builder. But the "basket" is full, and I send it forth knowing it will carry good cheer and blessing to some homes and hearts, and, I trust, to many.   H. A. T.

HUDSON, WIS., *February, 1874.*

LUTE A. TAYLOR.

LUTE A. TAYLOR was born in Norfolk, St. Lawrence county, New York, September 14th, 1835. His father died when Lute was but eight years of age, leaving his mother, with a family of five children, in destitute circumstances. He was, therefore, from his early boyhood, compelled to a life of toil. He earned with his own hands the means to support himself, and to acquire a thorough academical education. He very early gave evidence of excellent literary taste and abilities.

In the fall of 1856 he moved to River Falls, Pierce county, Wisconsin, and in June of the following year he issued the initial number of his first newspaper — the "River Falls Journal." In the spring of 1861 he removed the "Journal" office to Prescott, Wis., where, until 1869, he published the "Prescott Journal." In August, 1869, he entered upon a broader field of journalism, becoming one of the publishers and the editor-in-chief of the La Crosse "Morning Leader." This position he filled until a few months prior to his death.

In his career as an editor he was distinguished by a keen wit, a bright and vigorous style, and great range of subjects. His fame was justly high, and his ability was well known and appreciated by a wide circle of readers.

Mr. Taylor was appointed Assistant Assessor of Internal Revenue, on the organization of that bureau of service, and very soon after, on the 1st of January, 1864, he received the appointment as Assessor of the Sixth Congressional District of Wisconsin, and continued in that office until its abolition, in the spring of 1873. On the designation of La Crosse as a port of entry, in the summer of 1873, Mr. Taylor was appointed surveyor of the port, which position he held at the time of his death.

Mr. Taylor died at his home in La Crosse, Wis., of congestion of the lungs, after an illness of a week, on the 11th day of November, 1873.

It is surely an easy task to praise a friend, but to praise him wisely is not easy. There are a great many who loved Lute A. Taylor looking on as I write, and their affection for him will make them severe critics. They will hardly let the right intention excuse poor work. Nevertheless, as he was generous himself, it may be hoped that his friends are generous also, and that they will read "the lines between the lines," and so fulfill that which is lacking in this attempt.

The most of those who will read these words knew him by thought, if not by sight. He had a wide acquaintance, as the sorrow at his death has made known. It seems that those who did know him nearly, were apt to speak of him to others.

There are people whom you meet and forget instantly, who speak, and no one listens — people with the minus sign — nothing to give. If you remember them at all, it is that they have borrowed something. Lute Taylor had life, and that abundantly; threw off light and heat like a sun. Men remembered that they had met him, and his sayings did not pass away. "His presence was a festival." He lifted one out of a low mood on to rising ground. Men caught courage and good cheer by contact with him. He reconciled one to being human. "Bright is the sun, O Frenchman, when thou comest to visit us!" said the Chief of the Illinois to Pere

Marquette.   Our friend had this power to brighten a dull landscape, to let the light in and chase away the shadows. Nature made him a welcome guest in the homes and hearts of men.

The evening of his lecture, perhaps, was stormy, and the people gathered together might have been wet outside and gloomy within.   He cured all that in five minutes.   It was something like what was done at the wedding at Cana of Galilee.   He began with a benediction; there was a color and "bead" in what he said that restored the circulation. Men with blank faces, rayless of expression since childhood, felt the blood coming to the surface, and began to look human with laughter and tears.   It was worth a good deal to see this smiting of the rock and to find that it was moist at the center.

Taylor was a natural man, sinless of the self-consciousness that murders so many.   He lost himself in the theme of his discourse, and in the melody he chanted was able to put his purpose above himself.   It is a rare gift; without it there is no easy attitude, or free, brave stroke possible.   I think that Taylor saved more of his childhood than most men — was not spoiled by life.   If he failed to learn our prudence, he also neglected to acquire our suspicion and miserable doubt of all the good we see.   He died without making this grievous gain that costs us a good deal to get, and makes us sorry to keep.   Taylor was one of those who, when they die, make the world seem thinly inhabited.   He was not as other men are.   The majority of all who have lived to middle age have declared that there was no use in it — that life was a barren errand, no gain in doing it, except weariness.   Perhaps they all started with a purpose to pick berries for market, but before noon they looked in the pail, and had so few, that they concluded that they might as well eat them, and

did it, and so have gone home ashamed. Thoreau says that
" the boy gathers materials for a temple, and then, when he is
thirty, concludes to build a woodshed." We are, most of us,
acquainted with that boy. We shall see him putting his head
on his hand, and thinking of his childish purpose — the beauty
of it, and, alas! the vanity of it. That he should ever have
thought to have kept a sentiment in such a world as this!
Then he ceases to grow, and begins to wither and to shrink.

> "In his heart is the wind of Autumn,
> And the first fall of the snow."

There are signs that navigation is about to close. The
generous impulse and ready belief of youth are being frozen in; the fire is going out. Once in a while the Rachel
within lifts up a lament for the slain children of hope, but
more and more faintly; there are plenty of worldly maxims to
hush her with.

But there was one among us who had not made this fail-
ure and fall. Our friend had kept his heart. " Blessed are
they that hear the joyful sound." Taylor had an ear for it,
detected it, where we hear only the doleful. How quick was
his recognition, how prompt his praise of anything good in
the work of his fellows!

In a little book called "Back-Log Studies," there is a
pleasant picture. It is a day of winter storm; wild snow-
drifts blown against the windows of the cellar kitchen of a
farm house. A boy sits in the chimney-corner reading about
Burgoyne and the Indian wars. " John," says the mother,
"you'll burn your head to a crisp in that heat." But John
does not hear. He is storming the plains of Abraham just
now. "Johnny, dear, bring in a stick of wood." How can
Johnny bring in wood when he is in that defile with Braddock,
and the Indians are popping at him from behind every tree?

The childhood of Taylor was in the days of the back-log, the forestick, and the tallow candle. Days of the stage driver, and of Walter Scott's novels. There was little to read, and that little was good. Luke's " Lives of Saints," and Plutarch's " Lives of Heroes." I think something of the charm of his manner, and quaintness of his speech, was due to these early associations. He was old-fashioned. The memory of the old stories read in the firelight was very bright in him, and gave his conversation the glow of the early time, when we did not have to import a man from Switzerland, in order to possess one who had "no time to make money."

I believe that the impediment in his speech was a blessing to it — delayed it, as the drawing of a bow delays the arrow. It was as a dam ; when the sentence broke over, it fell in power of volume to turn the wheel of the mill, and in beauty of spray to please the eye of the miller.

I believe that if you "improve" the trout brook, by picking the rocks out of its bed, and by straightening its channel, you will be sorry. Let every man glory in his infirmities. Hindrances help — the kitemaker knows it, and God knows it, and makes his men according, giving them weights to carry.

I do not know that I can prove to a stranger and an un-believer that Taylor was a man of genius. I believe that all who knew him felt that he was. The work that some men are permitted to do is greater than they are. We trace the works of Shakspeare back to the poor player, and cannot so account for them. And again, some men are greater than their work; what they do is only a sign. Taylor was never brought into action. There were reserves in him that were never called to the front. He died, leaving a mass of unfinished business. He thought that life was a long summer day. It was not, for him, even a short winter day. Who thought

that he would be called at noon? So with him, the morning
was used in doing chores, in going on necessary errands;
perhaps he was gone longer than was necessary; also, in
chatting with the neighbors who dropped in, the time flew
by, and the day for him was done.

We miss the master; he is gone, leaving few designs
drawn on the trestle-board. We believe they were drawn in
his mind, and that he had the power and will to build according to them, and make his works his witnesses.

It is not easy to *enter* on a literary career — easy enough,
if fortunate, to continue it. We *must* do some things before
we can sit down to a task that is done on such long time as
one's first literary work.

The question of "bread" does come in. Burns must
plow the daisy under, and then, if he has *time*, he can lift it
up to bloom in a poem immortal — an unfading flower of a
not transient summer.

I take little stock in the present blessing said to be dis-
guised in poverty. It may work out something for us
hereafter, but in the life that now is, it is a good deal of a
curse. It consumes the days of youth, and postpones the
task that has no money in it to the days that may come, and
find us in no mood for working worthily, or past all work,
dead under the snow.

If we were assured a reasonably long life, we could, perhaps, afford to spend thirty or forty years in fighting, and
slaying, and burying past all resurrection the wolf at the
door, and then go in, and still have time to do the thing we
want to do.

As it is, the life is worn away in getting a living, and
there is little or nothing over. The miller has taken the grist
for toll. The fate that sets Burns to plowing is as an Indian
who makes an arrow-head out of a diamond.

The man of whom I am writing had no complaint of this kind to *make*. I make it for him. He bided his time—earned a book, and looked into it, and laid it down, to go to work at anything that offered; cut his own way, made his own clearing. So it is that there is so little of what he has done in the line of his genius. His common conversation was evidence enough of the unwrought wealth that lay under. What was carelessly tossed up on the surface was a sufficient sign.

He was thoroughly human, and so had faults. But, if the flaws had all been ground down, and ground out, he would still be of rare size. His faults were of the kind that make us sorry and not angry. With great gifts come great dangers. Lute Taylor was not what he ought to have been; but when you told him so, it was no news to him; it was a thought familiar enough. Some men need a logical argument to convince them that they are sinners. They are so prudent and sly in concealing their sin from others that they forget where it is themselves. Taylor was not of that kindred; never numbed and discouraged his conscience by disputing its voice, but confessed judgment.

An extract from Carlyle's words, concerning another, expresses the truth of him: "Who is called the man after God's own heart? David, the Hebrew king, had fallen into sins enough; there was no want of sin, and, therefore, unbelievers sneer, and ask, Is this your man according to God's heart? The sneer, I must say, seems to me but a shallow one. What are faults, what are the outward details of a life, if the inner secret of it, the remorse, temptations, the often baffled, never ended struggle of it, be forgotten? David's life and history, as written for us in those Psalms of his, I consider the truest emblem ever given us of a man's moral progress and warfare here below. All earnest souls will ever discern in it the faithful struggle of an earnest human soul toward what is good and best. Struggle often baffled — sore baffled, driven as into entire wreck! Yet a struggle never ended — ever with tears, repentance, true, unconquerable purpose — begun anew."

There is, O reader! sin, and sin: we must distinguish between the sin of impulse, the outward stain, and that which dyes the soul in the grain. The outcast girl of the street is forgiven. The whip of cords is braided for the respectable trader who has an office in the temple. Envy, malice, uncharity — these are of the brood who gnaw from within out — leave the man hollow to the whitewash. Of this generation of serpents, the heart of Lute Taylor knew nothing.

We must make the distinction, for it is wide. Richard Yates, in his last speech, after alluding to the way sundry Christian statesmen once had of using him, and his infirmity to point a moral, and then calling attention to the late appearance of the names of these brethren in the "little memorandum book" of Oakes Ames, said: "My friends and neighbors, I want you to remember that if my hand does tremble, it is *clean*."

Nature forbids some people to be generous in judgment; but there is always a chance for an attempt to be just. There's a choice in sinners. We rather have the prodigal son for a neighbor than his elder brother. And I judge from the parable that we agree with Christ. Let us look at one another "at our best," and believe that so we shall all appear at our last.

The face of Lute Taylor is before me as I write. None more kindly under the sun. Children believed in it, and old men. You can't deceive instinct and experience both. You can't wear a good face thirty-eight years without the help of a good heart. The lines are graven from within. There is no beauty at that age, except the beauty of thought. The fashion that it wears reveals the taste of the spirit.

"Thoughts of youth are long, long thoughts," sings Long-fellow. It seems so. The chief book of Taylor's childhood in his last days again took its place. Being asked, "What shall I read to you?" he answered, "Something from Paul. I want something that has *meat* in it." And so was read to him that wonderful fifteenth chapter of Paul's first letter to the Corinthians.

With these words for his company — rod and staff to comfort him in his journey through the valley of the shadow of death — we have, in sorrow and hope, bidden him "ADIEU," and "TILL WE MEET AGAIN."

2

LUTE TAYLOR'S CHIP·BASKET.

A LECTURE.

MARGARET FULLER.

MARGARET FULLER.

MARGARET FULLER OSSOLI is the most noteworthy and remarkable woman whom America has produced. Without scepter, or crown or throne, she was still a queen. Into whatever circle she came, she was its central figure; always the inspiring teacher, the wise counselor, the faithful friend. It is now but twenty years since the remorseless waves of the Atlantic swallowed up all of her that was mortal, yet she already wears the luster of an historic name. Her pictures do not line our albums, nor hang upon our parlor walls, yet her influence is wide and widening and her fame is assured.

Women sometimes win an enduring place in history, and are welcomed into the warm regard and affection of the world, simply because they are the wives of eminent men. It is doing no discredit to the honorable name of Martha Washington to say, that in almost every American town there are women who, in natural endowment and variety of achievement, are her equals at least. It was the relation in which she stood to the great man who is the central figure of our early history, that has made her

name a household word wherever the English language is spoken, and, with a few notable exceptions,
it is to a similar cause that other well known American women owe their prominence.

It was not thus with Margaret Fuller.   She rose
to her position of eminence by the unaided force
of her own great achievement.   She ruled in her
own right, and there was none to dispute her title to
the queendom ; and the fact that her life and history
may not be familiar to the mass of her countrymen
and countrywomen, detracts nothing from the splendor of her genius, and will only retard, but not
defeat, its final recognition.

There are thoughts which are germinal thoughts;
there are minds whose conceptions are so large,
and whose logic is so severe; that they must be
interpreted into common phrase before they are
universally accepted and understood.   Thus the
beauties of Solomon's Song, or the almost equally
divine sonnets of Shakspeare, are often unrecognized
until they dribble out to us, one beauty at a time,
in the verse of lesser poets.   So the great writers
upon political economy reach the people mainly as
their ideas are retailed out in articles of the newspaper press.

It is, fortunately, not necessary to the enjoyment
of thoughts or fancies that we should know to whom
we are indebted for them.   In the sweet summer
time the air of city courts and country lanes is
musical with the songs of love, and the enjoyment
of the singers is no less perfect and complete be-

cause they do not know from whence the sentiment and the melody have come. In this manner the songs of Burns fill all the earth, and, in like manner, the thoughts of Margaret Fuller inspire and control very many who do not know to whom they owe their impulse and their inspiration.

The time of her advent marked a new era in American life and literature. She was one of those who gave to scholarship a broader culture; to speculation, freer play; to philosophy, a bolder range; to religion, a firmer faith. The sermons of Channing and Clarke, the essays of Emerson, the romance of Hawthorne, and the editorials of Greeley, were alike colored by contact with her masterful mind.

Great as she was in the domain of intellect, her mind did not dwarf her heart. Always the true, noble, loving woman, seeking truth at whatever sacrifice, and accepting it at whatever cost, in her work of severe self-culture she never forgot the struggles of others, or neglected to reach them a helping hand. How broad and catholic her sympathies were, may be inferred from the following passage, taken from one of her earlier poems:

> "Happy are all who reach that crystal shôre,
>   And bathe in heavenly day;
> Happiest are they who high the banner bore,
>   To marshal others on the way;
> Or waited for them, fainting and wayworn
>   By burthens overborne."

I apprehend that in this day of universal suffrage —this day of deification of the people— when nu-

merical majority is made the test of truth, and
success the criterion of merit,—that it will do us
good to turn from the contemplation of the dead
level of the masses, and lift our eyes to meet the
radiance of some surpassing life. We need to cool
our admiration of majorities by a little devout and
reverent hero worship. "*Vox populi vox Dei*" is one
of the most subtle forms of falsehood with which
the devil ever calmed the fervor of noble aspiration
or choked the utterance of struggling truth. The
voice of the people is *not* the voice of God, unless
it be a Godlike people who speak. That voice is
more often audible to us only when echoed back
from the understanding hearts of the saints and
sages of the time—only when translated into the
lives and words of such rare and gifted souls as she
of whom I speak to you.

It is necessarily the lot of most of us to be engaged in other than intellectual pursuits. We are
not brought by our daily walk into contact with
sages and poets; we win our bread from an earth
whose mysteries are not open to us; our daily intercourse is more likely to stifle than encourage the
sparks of love and faith in our breasts, and so there
is the more necessity that we keep alive within us
the conviction of the divinity of our origin and the
possibilities of our future by a reverent study of the
words and deeds of those who have lived on the
mountain heights of human experience, and faced
two worlds at once.

Margaret Fuller was born in Cambridgeport, Mass.,

in 1810. Her father was educated at Harvard, and was a lawyer and a politician. She speaks of him as being largely endowed with that sagacious energy which New England society was so well fitted to develop. The great object of his ambition was to hold an honored place among his fellow men, and provide a comfortable and pleasant home for his family.

Of her mother she says: "She was one of those fair and flower-like natures which sometimes spring up beside the most dusty highways of life — a creature not to be shaped into a merely useful instrument, but bound by one law to the blue sky, the dew, and the frolic birds. Of all persons I have ever known, she had in her most of the angelic — of that spontaneous love for every living thing — for man and beast and tree,— which restores the golden age."

Margaret early gave proof of her wonderful power. Her father was proud of her, and stimulated her mind to over-work. At six years of age she read Latin with ease. As she thoroughly understood the mechanism of the language, she was required to give the thought in the briefest and best arranged language possible. Thus her mind was early trained to work with clearness and precision; but this forcing process told fearfully on her health. The poetic, dreaming element, strong in every child, was doubly strong in her, and she became the victim of nervousness, and the whole state of her being was painfully active and intense. It was a wonder to the family

that she was never willing to go to bed, but, using
her own language, "they did not know that as
soon as the light was taken away she seemed to see
colossal faces advancing slowly towards her, the eyes
dilating, and each feature swelling loathsomely as
they came, till at last, when they were about to close
upon her, she started up with a shriek, which drove
them away, but only to return when she lay down
again.   They did not know that when she went to
sleep it was to dream of horses trampling over her,
and to wake in fright, as she had just read in her
Virgil, of being among trees that dropped with
blood, where she walked and walked, and could not
get out, while the blood became a pool and plashed
over her feet, and soon she dreamed it would reach
her lips.   No wonder the child arose and walked in
her sleep, moaning, over the house, till once they
came and waked her; and when she told what she
had been dreaming of, her father sharply told her
to 'leave off thinking of such nonsense, or she would
be crazy,' never dreaming that he was himself the
cause of all these horrors of the night."

But these spectral illusions wore away; the tone
of her mind became more healthy, and study ceased
to be task work.

When fifteen years of age, she gives the following
account of her studies:

"I rise a little before five, walk an hour, and then
practice on the piano until seven, when we breakfast.   Next I read French — 'Sismondi's Literature
of the South of Europe' — till eight; then two or

three lectures in 'Brown's Philosophy.' About half-past nine I go to Mr. Parker's school and study Greek till twelve, when, school being dismissed, I recite, go home and practice again until dinner, at two. Sometimes, if the conversation is very agreeable, I lounge for half-an-hour over the dessert, though rarely so lavish of time. Then, when I can, I read two hours in Italian, but I am often interrupted. At six I walk, or take a drive. Before going to bed, I play or sing for half-an-hour or so, to make all sleepy, and, about eleven, retire to write a little while in my journal, or a series of characteristics, which I am fitting up according to advice. Thus, you see, I am learning Greek and making acquaintance with metaphysics and French and Italian literature."

At twenty years of age, she was again in Cambridge, and beneath the shadows of venerable Harvard. She was gladly welcomed into equal companionship with the strongest thought and ripest culture of the day. She had wealth and wisdom to give as well as to receive.

*   *   *   *   *   *

It is not necessary to dwell upon the details of her life, which, until her visit to Europe, was barren of exciting interest, as the lives of scholars and thinkers usually are.

Her occupation was divided between teaching, writing for the press — the New York "Tribune" mainly — and authorship; but, wherever placed, she was an intellectual magnet, drawing to herself all that was rare in culture and rich in intellectual endowment.

She combined the splendor of power and the possession of intellect with the grace of youth and the charm of womanhood, and was at once a personal impulse and an intellectual inspiration in the lives of such men as Clarke, Channing, Ripley, Greeley and Emerson.

It was in conversation that her mind found freest play and most congenial occupation. James Freeman Clarke says: ·

"She did many things well, but nothing so well as she talked. For some reason or other she could never deliver herself in print as she did with her lips. Her conversation I have seldom heard equaled. Though remarkably fluent and select, it was neither fluency nor choice diction, nor wit nor sentiment, that gave it its peculiar power; but accuracy of statement, keen discrimination, and a certain weight of judgment, which contrasted strongly and charmingly with the youth and sex of the speaker."

Emerson says of her evening conversations, when she was a visitor at his house:

"They interested me in every manner; talent, memory, wit, stern introspection, poetic play, religion, the finest personal feeling, the aspects of the future; each followed each in full activity, and left me, I remember, enriched, and somewhat astonished by the gifts of my guest. Her topics were numerous, but the cardinal points of poetry, love and religion, were never far off."

Possessed of this wonderful magnetic power, able to startle, charm or convince at will, it is no wonder that her friends were warmly attached to her, and she to them. So tender was her affection that she made her friends' souls her own, and, like a guardian genius, identified herself with their fortunes. She was everywhere a welcome guest. Her arrival was a holiday, and so was her abode. With her broad web of relations to so many noble friends, she seemed like the queen of some parliament of love, who carried the key to all confidences, and to whom every question was finally referred; and yet there was so much of intellectual aim and activity breathed through her alliances, as to give a dignity to them all. Channing says of her: "She was indeed the friend. This was her vocation. Into whatever home she entered, she brought a benediction of truth, justice, tolerance and honor. She knew, if not by experience, then by no questionable intuition, how to interpret the inner life of every man and woman, and by interpreting she could soothe and strengthen. To associates, her presence seemed to touch even common scenes and daily cares with splendor, as when, through the scud of a rain-storm, sunbeams break from serene blue openings, crowning familiar things with glory. To sustain the intimate personal relations which she did to so many representative men of her time, was a higher privilege than has ever fallen to the lot of any other American woman.

"There are many people who talk as if there were but two extremes of relation which woman can sustain to man. She must be a pretty, tricky, artful creature, beguiling him of his reason, taking him captive through his senses, the panderer to his pleasures, at once his tyrant and his slave ; or she must arm herself against him, accuse him, abuse him, as at once the sole author of her wrongs, the source of all her miseries. The fair, open land between the serene and sacred land of friendship, where men and women may meet in human sympathy, in kindred pursuits, in wide thoughts and in beneficent action, we hear constantly spoken of as a debatable, if not an impossible, meeting-ground. It, doubtless, is for the people who express this opinion, but it never has been, and never will be, for those men and women who recognize and revere in each other the equal human nature which each receive from God. Always man needs woman to be his friend. He needs her clearer vision, her subtler insight, her swifter thought, her winged soul, her pure and tender heart. Always woman needs man to be her friend. She needs the vigor of his purpose, the ardor of his will, his calmer judgment, his braver force of action, his reverence and his devotion. Thus the mystic bond of sex, which binds one half the universe in counterpart and balance to the other, gives even to the friendship of man and woman its finest charm, enabling each, only through the other, to preserve the perfect equipoise of intellect and soul. Such a friend was Margaret Fuller to the men who still speak her name with reverent tenderness."

As a writer, she was critical rather than creative. Her published works are, "Summer on the Lakes," "Papers on Literature and Art," "Woman in the Nineteenth Century," and more valuable, perhaps, than either of these, the extracts from her journals and letters, which her biographers have preserved. Her last and greatest work perished irrevocably in the wreck which closed her earthly career; but some idea of its fire and force can be gathered from passages in her letters from Italy, which are preserved and presented in her memoirs.

Her "Papers on Literature and Art" are among the most valuable contributions to American criticism. Her review of Longfellow's poems startled, if it did not convince, the world of letters; and no one has ever dissected the nature and stated the effect of Byron's poems, with so clear an insight and so truthful a discrimination, as she has done. It is especially interesting to note the estimation in which Margaret Fuller held the author of " Childe Harold," and the rank among poets to which she assigns him.

Byron's life was both a tragedy and a farce. He was essentially an actor. A vein of insincerity pervades all his poems. His thin mask of levity does not hide the skepticism which lies uneasy and sorrowful beneath it; nor when his misanthropic fit is on does his sorrow strike us as very earnest and real. He would have us believe that his richest wines were powdered with the dust of graves; yet he frequently took more of that wine than was good for him. It was in the winter of 1814, while dis-

robing after balls, haunted, in all probability, by
eyes in whose light he was happy enough, that he
wrote his " Lara," and pictured death as

"That sleep the loveliest, since it dreams the least."

This was meant to take away the reader's breath,
and, no doubt, after penning it, Byron betook himself to bed with a sense of supreme cleverness; yet,
contrasted with Shakspeare's far-out-looking and
thought-heavy lines, where death is represented by
the same image, it glitters like tinsel instead of shining like gold.

Margaret Fuller speaks of Byron's poems as his-
torically valuable as records of that strange malady,
that sickness of the soul, which cankers so visibly
the rose of youth. This sickness of feeling finds
its highest water-mark in him. He has lived through
this experience for us — has shown that the natural
fruits of indulgence in such a temper are not to be
desired; and, as grief loses half its fascination when
we find that others have endured the same and lived
through it, so, she thinks the evil has been greatly
lessened since he has so fully illustrated it. This is
but a bold exhibit of what she states with logical
exactness and convincing force.

As an illustration of the clearness of her thought
and the felicity of her expression, I give her defini-
tion of an epic, as contrasted with an occasional
poem:

"An epic, a drama, must have a fixed form in the
mind of the poet from the first, and copious draughts

of ambrosia, quaffed in the heaven of thought; soft, fanning gales, and bright light from the outward world, give muscle and bloom — that is, give life to the skeleton. But occasional poems must be moods, and a mood cannot have a form fixed and perfect, any more than a wave of the sea."

Margaret Fuller was a radical. I like that word radical. It stirs the blood like a challenge to arms. The radicals are the trumpeters of truth. They people the picket lines of progress. Margaret Fuller, I repeat, was a radical — not a blind iconoclast, ruthlessly attacking cherished forms and customs which have crystallized into laws, but a wise prophet, who, seeing a fairer future beckoning to us, patiently but persistently strove to clasp its outstretched hands. She did not believe that customs and laws were set up as barriers to progress, but rather that they are tents of a night upon the camping-ground of life, to be struck whenever truth puts the bugle to her lips and sounds an advance. Wrong, though rooted in antiquity and fortified by innumerable precedents, gained no homage from her; but right found her a faithful follower, however few its followers might be. She clearly discerned the injustice of social and the iniquity of political life, and the fire of her indignation burned fiercely against oppression and villainy in every form. We must remember that many of the asperities of law have been softened in the last twenty-five years; that when she talked and wrote the sphere of woman was much more restricted than now; that slavery then defiled the land with its

3

presence, burdened it with its sin, and darkened it · with the gloom of threatened disaster.

None saw the magnitude of legally organized cruelty more clearly than she; none had a firmer faith that the day of deliverance would come. She saw, with the poet,

> "Right forever on the scaffold,
> Wrong forever on the throne."

but she believed, with him,

> Yet that scaffold sways the future, and behind the dim un-
>   known
> Standeth GOD, within the shadow, keeping watch above his
>   own.

The movement called, for want of a better name, the Woman's Rights movement, found one of its pioneers and its most powerful champions in her. She threw down the gauntlet with an air of knightly defiance. Almost alone in her convictions, she startled timidity and shocked conservatism by exclaiming of women, "Let them be sea captains, if they will." Her "Woman in the Nineteenth Century" is the most powerful plea which has ever been made for putting woman on a par, politically, with man, and it required a good deal of valor to stand unmoved amid the shower of public squibs and private sneers called out by her demand. Now it is getting fashionable to espouse this cause; she defended it in its despised infancy.

More than a quarter of a century ago she wrote: " Let man trust woman entirely, and give her every

privilege already acquired for himself—elective franchise, tenure of property, and liberty to speak in public assemblies. Nature has pointed out her ordinary sphere by the circumstances of her physical existence. If here and there the gods send their missives through women as through men, let them speak without remonstrance.   *   *   *   *
Neither let men fear to lose their domestic deities. Woman is born for love, and it is impossible to keep her from seeking it. Man should deserve her love as an inheritance, rather than seize and guard it like a prey."

Others may have felt as keenly as she the injustice to woman, imbedded in our social polity and ideas, but there was no other one so fitted by thought, by culture, by position, and by fearlessness, to discuss the subject thoroughly and present the argument in its amplest proportions. Much that has been accomplished in enlarging the sphere and increasing the opportunities of women, is justly due to her initial labors; and now, when the time seems to be approaching when woman will be called upon calmly and authoritatively to decide for herself whether the ballot is too rude and perilous a weapon for her delicate hand, the words of Margaret Fuller will be consulted, not more deferentially, but far more widely, than they have hitherto been.

Candor compels me to confess that while I cannot break the force of her logic upon this subject, neither can I accept all of its conclusions. And, I believe, that in later years, when a husband wore her

wifely love as a jewel, and her low lullaby stilled
the clamor of her baby boy, there was then wrought
in her philosophy something of the change which
was wrought in Tennyson's "Princess," when love,
the magician, touched her with his all-conquering
wand.

A woman without religion is a star without radiance — a flower without perfume.   It is interesting,
therefore, to note the religious character of Margaret
Fuller.

I think I have never read of a person more pro-
foundly religious than she.   Her journals, her letters
and her life are full of humility, piety and prayer.
The fact that she was the intimate friend of Emerson, that she was closely connected with the movements of the Transcendentalists in New England —
that for two years she edited the "Dial," the organ
of that party — led a good many good orthodox
people to doubt the soundness of her religious experience.   A transcendentalist she was, in the full
meaning of the word.   Her religion did indeed
transcend the religion of commoner and meaner
minds.   She was a "pilgrim from the idolatrous
world of creeds and rituals, to the temple of the
living God in the soul."   "The peaceful benediction
of heaven sounded forth to her in flowers and stars;
in the poetry, art and heroism of all ages; in the
aspirations of her own spirit, and in the budding
promise of the time."   That religion which looks
reverently to God, and lovingly upon man — that
religion which cares for the temporal as well as the

eternal good of our fellows — that religion which permeates every path of life, and sheds a sacred light on every duty — that religion which knows the sorrow that ever springs from earth and feels the consolation which descends to meet it from above — that religion which walks the ways of life in close companionship with the invisible form of one like unto the Son of Man; that religion was Margaret Fuller's. Horace Greeley says of her: "I never met another being in whom the aspiring hope of immortality was so strengthened into profoundest conviction. She did not *believe* in a future and unending state of existence — she *knew* it, and lived in the full splendor of its dawning light."

In the spring of 1846, rich in experiences, rich in culture, and rich in friends, heralded by her reputation as a scholar and writer, Margaret departed for Europe. She was cordially received in England, and found ready access to such society as that of Wordsworth, DeQuincy, Dr. Chalmers, Carlyle, Mary Howitt, Joanna Baillie, and others like them. Here, too, she first met Joseph Mazzini, the Washington of Italy, and here began that acquaintance which, amidst the subsequent storms of the Italian revolution, ripened into congenial confidence and sacred trust.

In December she went to Paris, where the best literary society was open to her, and she became the friend of George Sand and Berenger. Here she had frequent opportunities of hearing the great actress, Rachel, and her criticisms are almost as

grand as a tragedy.   She says of Rachel's eye : " It
was magnificent to see the dark cloud give out such
sparks, each one fit to deal a separate death."

In May, 1847, she went to Rome.   She was warmly
welcomed by the distinguished Americans resident
there, and found easy access to the best native
society.

Here a new world opened to her.   From infancy
the Roman character had been the object of her
admiration.   Rome was to her a magic word.   The
Roman was an emperor.   The dignity of command,
the inflexible purpose of will, was stamped upon him.

Here in the most obscure places the spirits of the
mighty dead crowded upon her ; here the old kings,
the consuls, the emperors, the warriors of eagle eye
and remorseless beak returned to her ; the toga-clad
procession swept across the scene ; innumerable
temples glittered, and the *Via Sacra* swarmed with
triumphal life once more.   Here, too, a new world
of love opened to her, and she found that

> "Tradition, snowy-bearded, leaned
> On romance, ever young."

Going, one evening, with a party of friends, to
attend vespers at St. Peter's, at the close of the service she became separated from her companions.
After anxiously seeking for them some time, she was
accosted by a young Italian, who politely asked if he
could assist her.   Failing to find her friends, he went
to call a cab, but they had all departed, and he ac-
companied her home.   That courtly stranger was

OSSOLI, and, a short time after, Margaret became his bride. Ossoli was of princely lineage, his family being one of the oldest in Rome. Himself a Liberal, his brothers were in the papal service. His father was dead, and the estate was unsettled. Ossoli wished to keep the marriage a secret until his affairs were arranged, lest the fact of his union with a Protestant should deprive him of his property.

Margaret, some time after, removed to Rieti, where she became a mother. Of her child, the boy Angelo, it would be almost profane to repeat her words of praise. Of Ossoli, she says, " He is capable of the sacred love — the love passing that of woman. He has shown it to his father, to Rome and to me." ·

Meanwhile the war-cloud broke, and the revolution of 1848 arrested the attention of the world. Of that lost struggle of Italy, she might not merely say, with the Grattan of Ireland's kindred effort half a century earlier, " I stood by its cradle — I followed its hearse," but she might fairly claim to have been a portion of its incitement, its animation, its informing soul. Her husband was an officer in the Republican army, and she bore more than a woman's part in its conflicts and its perils. Whether in council chamber with the chiefs, or in hospital wards with the dying, she was always helpful, untiring, resolute and brave; and when at last, through the perfidy of a traitorous government, the dearest hopes of the people were drowned in blood, there was no heart more lofty in its defiance, no voice more eloquent in its exposure of the villainy, than her own.

Weary in spirit, with the deep disappointments of the past year weighing heavily upon her, she spent the winter of 1849–50 in Florence.   Here she was surrounded by a pleasant circle of American and English friends, and the last months of her Italian life were cheered by all the light that the presence of husband and boy and the companionship of gifted and noble natures could afford.

Here she wrote of Mazzini: "Mazzini is immortally dear to me—a thousand times dearer for all the trial I saw made of him at Rome—dearer for all that he suffered.   Many of his brave friends perished there.   We who, less worthy, survive, would fain make up for the loss by our increased devotion to him—the purest, the most disinterested of patriots, the most affectionate of brothers."

Beneath the ruins of the Roman Republic many private fortunes were swallowed up; and among them was Ossoli's, and he and Margaret decided to come to America.

Many motives conspired to draw Margaret back to her native land.   There was heart-weariness at the great reaction in Europe, desire of publishing her history of Italy—the fruit of her maturest thought—to the best advantage, and thereby doing justice to great principles and brave men, and the desire to be once more with youthful associates and family friends.

On the 17th of May, 1850, they embarked on the ship Elizabeth.

She trusted soon to greet loved ones on these

western shores. Alas! she knew not that another way was opened for her—

"To God's Eden-land, unknown."

The captain of the vessel was a model New England sailor, calm, courteous, brave; and his young wife, who was with him, was a lady, gentle and refined.

They had been at sea but a short time when the captain died of a malignant fever. Margaret's boy also sickened, but at length recovered, and sobered and saddened they could again hope, and enjoy the beauty of sea and sky. Margaret comforts the sorrowing widow, puts the last touches to her book on Italy, and sings and plays with her happy boy.

At noon on the 18th of July, the Elizabeth was off the Jersey coast, and the officer in command promised the passengers he would land them at New York in the morning. The weather was thick, the breeze strengthened into a tempest, the vessel made way with a rapidity no one dreamed of, and about 4 o'clock in the morning, she struck Fire Island beach, off the shore of Long Island.

I will not attempt to excite your feelings by a description of the awful scene which followed. The captain's widow and a few of the sailors were saved; but the chivalric husband, the excelling wife and the promising boy were swallowed up by the hungry sea. When last seen, Margaret was sitting at the foot of the foremast, still clad in her nightdress, with her hair fallen loose about her shoulders.

A great wave swept over the ship. It was over
—that communion face to face with death! It was
over—and the prayer was granted, that "Ossoli,
Angelo and I may go together, and that the anguish
may be brief."

This, then, O noble woman! was thy welcome
home. Instead of the clasp of affection and the
kiss of love—instead of high hopes realized and
large ambitions filled, there was an idle lifeboat, a
howling hurricane and a pitiless sea.

Truly, "He maketh darkness his pavilion round
about him—dark waters and thick clouds of the
skies."

But, though those clouds were tempest-torn and
black with death, we may yet fain believe that their
tops were golden in the sun, and through their broken
rifts we can almost see the splendor shining, and
hear a voice descending, saying with angelic accents,
"ALL IS LOST; BUT ALL IS WON."

THE CHIP BASKET.

[The most interesting department of Lute Taylor's paper, and the one in which he took the greatest pride, and loved most to labor, was his "Chip Basket." Here is what he said when he set it out for the first time, and asked his readers to assist in filling it, and test the flavor of its good cheer:]

CHIPS are not useless. The hewer cleaves them off, thinking only of the timber which assumes desired form by their removal, and the chopper thoughtlessly spins them from his gleaming axe — yet they have a value of their own. There is blessing and brightness in them. They glow cheerily in comfortable homes, and bring warmth to shivering squalor's scanty hearth.

Here we shall endeavor, week by week, to pick up the chips which the writers toss off at their toil, and make a pleasant warmth around which our readers will love to gather.

Pleasant paragraphs, little poems, bits of sentiment, reverie, philosophy, and speculation — fruits gathered from spice islands, passed in the sea of reading — these will be gathered here, to be enjoyed, we trust, by those who read.

Every newspaper reader knows there are favorite paragraphs which he meets with continually. They lead a curious, wandering life, sometimes going abroad triumphantly on the broad pages of a metropolitan paper, with an editorial preface, like a herald, to announce their presence, and again nestling unremarked in the narrow columns of some obscure and struggling sheet. Their authorship may be forgotten, their history unknown, but their life is assured. Broad and catholic in feeling, they depend on neither time nor place for interest, but speak to the universal heart of man. The melody of the breeze and the light of the stars, the beauty of day and the grandeur of night are in them, and they pass sentinel editors unchallenged, and keep their place in newspaper columns by inherent right. Many such we hope to gather and present in due season.

And the Chip Basket is wide, and will never be full. Our friends are invited to assist in the gathering. Around it will be the flavor of good cheer, of healthy sentiment, of kindly feeling, of a humor that may sparkle but will not sting.

RELIGION is the final center of repose, the goal to which all things tend, apart from which man is a shadow, his very existence a riddle, and the stupendous scenes of nature which surround him as unmeaning as the leaves which the sibyl scattered in the wind.

MEDITATION is to life what ballast is to a ship — to go safe and steady we must sometimes stop and think.

MIRAGE.

[Extract from a letter to a friend.]

In the days long ago, Frank, when you and I sat on hard benches at the district school house, wiggling on our seats like the fat worms which we impaled on our fish-hooks in the holidays — in those days when we studied Olney, we were taught that *mirage* was located on the great deserts. You remember how our boyish wonder was excited by the story of the travelers in the desert, weary, worn, seeking vainly for the saving spring, tortured beyond endurance by the hellish agonies of burning thirst, and how to their longing eyes there would sometimes come a vision beautiful as Paradise, a vision of cooling waters, of greenness and umbrage, and their eyes were lighted with new hope, and their weary feet strengthened with new vigor, as they pushed on toward the promised relief. But the taunting vision eludes their search, the mocking, impalpable oasis flees imperceptibly before them, and at last the cruel conviction is forced upon them that the pleasing picture is a phantom — and the horrid thirst burns fiercer, and the heart sinks in a deeper despair. This is *mirage*.

But the geographer forgot to tell us, what is equally true — that more mirage hangs deceitfully about political capitals than desert travelers ever saw. The hopes which cluster around these places are none the less high, the pursuit is none the less careful and intent, the disappointment is none the less bitter, the despair is none the less crushing and complete.

A man with compelling purpose, with tireless brain and an honorable ambition, fixes his heart on a desired place. Month after month and year after year he toils with indomitable perseverance, and unflagging zeal. At length the looked-for time arrives. Hopeful, almost exultant, he is sanguine of success, but a line from the executive, or the silent fall of bits of paper, and the prize struggled for with manly strength, coveted with intense desire, eludes his grasp, and the burning sands press not more pitilessly the blistered feet of the desert traveler than the world looks pitilessly upon the disappointment which has thwarted the cherished purpose of his life.

But not to political life alone does mirage lend its deceptive arts. The business man is often its victim; and over all the sky of youth it hangs its rosy colors, its pleasing tints, its glowing pictures of coming joys. The maiden, in the beauty and purity of a dawning womanhood, looks forward to a happy life of love, but

> "The cloud lands still before her lay,
> The mirage looms across her way;"

and the boy, eager for manhood, with its toils and triumphs, looks forward to a goal which he may never reach — a prize he may never win.

Blessed are they whose undoubting faith survives all disappointments, and from before whose hopeful eyes the mirage never fades away.

But when we look, Frank, to the rest beyond, where faith shall find its fulfillment, hope its fruition, and love its reward—when we look over to that other shore of life—perhaps wishing to be there, yet shrinking from the passage—when a vision of the loveliness of that land cools the fever, and calms the strife of our daily lives, can it be that the beauty which beckons us, and the smiling joys which reach out welcoming hands, are like the fair delusions here—a mirage and a cheat?

I do not believe it; and trusting that you, my boy, may find, at last, that the mirage of life here is but a reflection from the reality of life hereafter, I am very truly yours.

A NICKNAME.—The man who has won a nickname and wears it gracefully, has the elements of popularity about him. The same instinct which leads a mother to apply diminutive phrases of endearment to her little ones is a universal instinct, one which we never outgrow, and which continually manifests itself in our form of addressing or speaking of those we love, trust or admire.

The man who is known in his village or neighborhood as "Uncle" is never a cold, crabbed or selfish character. He is sure to have a generous heart, and wear a cheerful smile—there is integrity in him which men trust, and warmth around him which little children love to gather, and the term is a title of honor—more to be desired than that of "honorable."

FAT. — He is grand, stupendous, magnificent, sublime. In his imposing presence, in the great shadow of his rotund form, we are humility itself.

He is bigness personified.

He says his size and weight are a little unhandy. In sultry weather he feels too warm.

He used to walk up the steps into his office, but it has become too dangerous. At present he is brought from his house on a dray, lifted into the office with a derrick, and handled during the day with a cant-hook.

He was elected alderman. His ward is entitled to but three, and the other two have resigned.

He is taxed as real estate. The city assessor recently had him surveyed and platted, and he figured up six forties and several out-lots.

He is very large.

His wife has to get a new marriage certificate every little while, in order to keep her title to him perfect, and we fear she may be guilty of bigamy in being married to so much of mankind.

He really is fat.

He is growing rapidly.

THERE is no traveler equal to a good newspaper paragraph. Dr. Livingstone is not a circumstance in comparison. It gets lost and found, gets killed and revived, has its head taken off and a head put on, goes farther and often fares worse than any adventurer since the return of the heroes from the siege of Troy.

LOST MOTION.

A few days since we were talking with a skillful workman about repairing a large, valuable and complex piece of machinery. The practised eye of the quiet worker in iron readily discovered the causes of the defects of the great machine, and he expressed his perfect ability to remove them. Among other things, he said that the "lost motion must be taken up."

After the business was over we fell to thinking of his words, and wondering if most men and women —like deranged machinery—did not need to have lost motion taken up. The young man, starting in life with correct habits and good resolutions, yields step by step to the fascinations of indulgence and the seductions of sin, until every one sees that his moral powers have lost motion, which sadly needs to be taken up.

The man of middle life, whose trained and experienced powers are left to relax in idleness, or are used only for trifling, selfish, or unworthy purposes, has lost motion, and falls fearfully short of accomplishing the good which by nature he was fitted to do. The woman who, moving queen-like amid luxurious surroundings, or creating and sharing the comforts of a modest home, permits that home to be the boundary of her sympathies and care, and centers all her thought upon her own adornment, her pleasure, or her pride, unmindful of the pleading voices

4

of the poor, of the varied and innumerable forms which want and woe are constantly assuming, and which forever hem us in — she has lost motion in life, and, beautiful and radiant as she may be, falls far short of being the earthly angel which it is her privilege and duty to become. When we descend to lower grades of life, when blear-eyed vice and angry-visaged crime skulk in darkness, or deface the day, we find sights sadder still — ruins awful and complete.

The paralyzed conscience, the infirm will, and the unfeeling heart, are all indications of lost motion in life. Churches and chapels, lecture rooms and schools are workshops to which poor humanity repairs for the betterment of its condition — the restoration of the motion lost. How effective these agencies are, how many leave the church or chapel with feelings freshened, with conscience quickened, with faith strengthened, with purpose invigorated, and all the beauty and power and tension of life restored, it is not our purpose to inquire now.

GIT AND GUMPTION. — There are certain qualities of mind and character which, "down east," are described by the expressive words "*git*" and "*gumption.*" "Git," we take it, means a certain irresistible promptness and energy; and "gumption" a peculiar winning tact, something even better than industry and surer than genius. When "git" and "gumption" are combined the result is certain success.

TO A BOY EDITOR.

[The following is a letter written to Victor Welch, of Madison, Wisconsin, who, at the time the letter was written was under ten years of age, yet published a small paper at his father's residence :]

MASTER VICTOR JOHN WELCH:

A visit to the office of the "Home Diary," and the perusal of its files — a valued present from your father — has given me the ambition to write a letter for its pages, and thus join the choice circle of your contributors.

A printing office in a gentleman's private residence, with an editor whose years are expressed by a single figure, is at least an anomaly; but, in future years, when your pleased eye shall look over the pages of the "Diary," you will find, that although small in dimensions, in sprightliness of fancy, in incisive thought, in pungent criticism, it fairly rivals more ambitious sheets.

The types are wonderful things, Victor, and if, in learning to form them into lines and marshal them into columns, you also learn to use that wonderful instrument of power, the English language, with ease and accuracy and vigor, you will find that your father has given you a better "start in life" than if he had endowed you with stocks and bonds, or made you the owner of vast estates. Your name appears as editor of a paper at an age when a less favored

boy would perhaps feel the first promptings of ambition to secure this distinction.   In maturer years
you will more fully appreciate this honor, and will
perhaps translate into fact what is now a pleasing
fiction.

In my boyhood I often stood on the wharves of
one of our seaboard cities and saw the great ships
depart for far-off lands, and as they boldly stood out
upon the waste of waters, I wondered whether the
cruel, roaring, hungry sea would swallow them up,
or whether, after many months, they would return,
bringing wealth to their possessors, and happiness to
waiting hearts.   Just so, Victor, does a thoughtful
man regard a boy who is playing on the margin of
that sea of life across which he must boldly steer.

> "It may be that the gulfs will wash him down,
> It may be he will reach the Happy Isles."

None make the voyage in unbroken sunshine.
Storms will come, my boy, but Will and Work are
faithful pilots, and will bring you safely through.

In the years of your manhood, which is to come,
you will find that great hopes will die, great faiths
will be wrecked, great loves will be misdirected and
misplaced.   But you will also find that man is not
the powerless slave of nature or passion; if he cannot
imperatively rule, he can, at least, partially control
them both.   The sun goes down, but we light our
lamps and make a circle of brightness in the wide-
surrounding and close-pressing night; and so, when
the death of a great hope or the wrecking of a great

faith darken's life with love's eclipse, we may yet make it comfortable and serene by the aid of smaller joys, of lesser faiths, of homely duties faithfully performed.

It is easy to be advisory, Victor, and if this letter is didactic in its character, it will be but the common fault of men when writing to the young.

Your parents and teachers will impress on you the necessity of forming correct habits, but it is desirable that you early appreciate the almost omnipotent power of a habit when once it has obtained control of a man. I was once riding on a train of cars over a long reach of level prairie. Standing on the front platform of the rear car, the train running as if furies fed its fires, I noticed with surprise that the coupling which joined this car to the next was slack, and the car itself actually pushing on those before it. Only at intervals would the iron links straighten and the car feel the force of the ponderous engine which drew the train. You see, Victor, the car had got a *habit* of running—it had gathered momentum, and the same force which had put it in motion would have been powerless to arrest its course. Now, habit is simply momentum in a given direction of life. Its beginnings are slight, but its gathered, cumulative strength is almost beyond conception or belief. No rule can measure its force, no calculus determine its limit, no law control its power. It is a strong, imperious giant. It binds its victims with chains softer than silk, but stronger than steel. Impalpable, unseen, its power can fitly be compared to that invisible law of gravitation which binds the universe of God together, and controls the courses of the wandering worlds. One may well be awed in the presence of such power, and if you can but feebly estimate its strength, you will not need be admonished to be careful what habits you form.

As you grow older, Victor, you will be surprised at the paltry nature of the topics which engross many men's thoughts and fill their speech. The husks on which the Prodigal Son had nearly starved, were opulence itself compared to the mental pabulum on which so many fill their dwarfed, distorted minds. The small talk, the neighborhood gossip, the retailing of rumors, the rehearsal of unimportant events, the surmises and the speculations about other people's plans and purposes — these absorb the mental life of very many, and are at once the indication and the cause of barrenness of soul and poverty of mind. To the small things of your own life, and the lives of those with whom you live, give careful attention, for they are the friction in the machinery of life, but let the deluge of small talk which will surround you be as powerless to arrest your attention or disturb your repose, as the hail beating against closed blinds, is impotent to invade the security of the room within.

Another thing you will remember, Victor, that *character* is the most valuable part of a man. It is richer than wealth, better than brilliancy, grander than intellect. It is the besetting sin of youth to worship mere intellectual power. You will guard

against the fascination of this fault. A firmly established character is the only sure base on which a
noble superstructure can be reared. Great intellectual brilliancy or power, divorced from moral
worth, is like a marble shaft resting on shifting sand
—in the first tempest it will be overthrown, and lie
soiled upon the earth above which it should rise.
History and your own observation will teach you
that the lives of many of the most highly gifted are
valuable only as beacon lights to warn others of the
ruin in which they have been engulfed. A man
without character often achieves a seeming success,
but his triumph is transitory. Like the ungodly man
mentioned in Scripture, "Yet a little while and he
shall be clean gone ; thou shalt look after his place,
and he shall be away." A man with compelling brain,
with generous impulse and ready sympathy, with no
taint of meanness soiling his life, no canker of deceit
festering in his soul, whose convictions have crystallized into character, whose frank and fearless eye
beams a benediction on all of beauty and truth, and
flashes scorn on all of falsehood and pretense — such
a man is the " noblest work of God."

That you, Victor, may become such a man, each
day conferring blessing and enjoying content, until
the last day shall come, and you pass to the "other
side of life," where

> "Quiet reigns, and brings to brain and breast
>   The benediction of unbroken rest,"

is the sincere wish of your friend.

WOMAN'S RIGHTS. — Philosophers will some day
be called upon to decide why it is that the cause of
"Woman's Rights," which drags so painfully in the
old and thickly-settled East, has won its only signal
victories in the West.   We lack the courage, even if
we had the ability, to offer any suggestions toward
the solution of this question.   We know, of course,
that the light-minded and unreflecting would say
that it is because in the East the women outnumber
the men, while in the West that position is reversed;
but we are too well disciplined to say anything of
the kind — for that sort of statement implies too
grossly that the divinest half of creation is only
fully appreciated when it makes itself very scarce.
The weasel shall be entrapped in deep slumber
before our cautious pen assumes the guilt of such
villainy !   But the fact remains, and some day it will
puzzle the wiseacres.

OLD LETTERS. — Reader, have you a package of
letters from friends carefully tied with ribbon, or
safely laid in a private drawer. They are like a row
of tombstones in "God's Acre," marking the place
where friends have been laid.   They are dead now.
The soul passed out of them as you read them first,
and when you occasionally look over them now it is
for the same reason that you look at the picture of a
dead friend — to call up more vividly the memories
of the past.   As the life of those letters passed into
our own, so shall our lives one day pass into a greater
one.

A NIGHT IN A LIGHTHOUSE.

Years ago we were familiar with the murmuring of the sea, listened entranced to its wondrous voices, but it had been long since its music had been our lullaby and we had slept with its waters all around us. The sensation was almost novel and entirely delightful; we could not help thinking that we had some connection with the great light in the tower, and the safety which it gave to the sailors who passed by.

The sea has strange, multitudinous voices for those who have ears to hear. Sometimes it has a cry of pain, like it were a caged monster chafing at the bounds which confine it, and reaching out angrily to seize its prey; and again its tones are soft and seductive as the voices of the fabled sirens, and its retreating waves woo to their embrace with no intimation that their returning grasp is relentless as death. Sometimes the waves will thunder in a grand, joyful, and triumphant chorus, as if an omnipotent hand measured their flow into harmony with the melodies of infinite thought and the movements of limitless worlds; and again in fantastic and playful mood they will dance as lightly as the feet of Mirth, and sing as gayly as the lips of Love.

We seemed again to hear the sea in all these moods, and remembering the recent great storm, and the evidences of it which were all around us, the thought of its terror clung close to us, and in our fancy the wrecks drifted slowly by,

——" the gurgling cry
Of the strong swimmer in his agony"

fell upon our ears, and the drowned men came gliding
in procession before us, each spectral form now rising
on the crested wave and now dipping below it.

The thoughts became too heavy, and with sympathy for those who mourned the desolations which
shipwreck had made, and with thankfulness that such
sorrows had not invaded our life, we dismissed the
specters called up by fancy, and closing our ears to
the ceaseless voice of many waters, we slept soundly
in the lighthouse at Racine.

RAILROAD RIDING, even with pleasant compan-
ions, is tedious, unless one thinks, or rather *reveries*,
if that word can be used as a verb. It is so natural
for one to think that the train he is riding on is the
important train of that day. But if he stops to
think, he knows that all over the broad land, every
hour of the day and night, the great trains are shoot-
ing across States, as the shuttle shoots across the
loom, each filled with the same eager, expectant
throng. Each car-load is a small edition of the
great, surging, restless world. Some gaily intent on
pleasure; some on errands of business and gain;
some with hearts breaking with sorrow, hastening to
comfort the dying, or bury the dead; some on mis-
sions of mercy; some in the service of crime; some
hearts bright with climbing hopes which reach the
heavens; some dark with despair which shudderingly
recoils from hell.

THE NIGHT TRAIN.

There is something weird and almost ghostly about the shrieking passage of the night train over the long, level miles. Through the black night it goes, waking the stillness with its roar, and startling the darkness with the gleam of its rushing headlight, while its colored lanterns in the rear twinkle a hasty good-bye. It comes like a startling apparition — it goes like a dream of delirium, leaving one in wonder and amaze.

Within the train the sight is equally suggestive. Here are the employés faithful at their post, and the conductor moves about with ever watchful eye. Here is weariness, languor, and unconsciousness in every form. The strong man has forgotten his strength, and uneasily sits or lies in crumpled condition. The worn mother wearily tends her restless child, and snatches brief bits of sleep as the lazy hours creep slowly by. Here all is impatient waiting, discomfort and unrest; but back in the luxurious sleeping-car the unconscious inmates are wrapped in undisturbed repose, and unheeded by them the great train rushes on its way.

By and by the morning comes. Some with light hearts awake to feel its brightening touch rest like a benediction upon them. Others awake with aching heads and weary frames to face again the deep disappointment and the carking cares from which sleep had brought them only slight respite, and so all go on their several ways.

In the great journey of life there is a night train also. We shall all take it sometime. It is like the other of which we have written, in that there will be careful attendants around. The conductor on this train is the physician, who gives to us his constant, watchful care, while nurses and friends watch over us, obeying every order — as the brakesmen watch and control the movements of the rapid car. Here, too, are some tossing in the delirium of fever, writhing in the gripe of unrelaxing pain — while others, blest with unconsciousness, speed swiftly on to the journey's end.

To all these, also, the morning cometh; and they shall wake, like those others of whom we have written, as the night found them — some racked with remorse and scarred with sin — others bright with the splendors of unspeakable joy. When that night comes to us, may our passage be peaceful, our morning be unclouded day.

THE shining crystal snow is nothing but dark water purified by frost; and so the saintly souls we sometimes meet are only our common human nature sanctified by sorrow and sweetened by faith.

A MAN may be successful as a loafer, and invest less capital and brains than are required to succeed in any other profession.

"POOR CARLOTTA!"

On the 19th of June, in the city of Queretaro, in the fair sunlight of a beautiful day, guarded by legions of soldiers, and surrounded by a vast populace, a young and gallant gentleman was shot to death. He was of princely lineage, and his unshrinking courage and noble mien well became his royal birth and blood.

Standing there in the awful moment which was to divide two worlds, his thoughts were not of hopes ruined, of honors lost, of ambitions crushed or confidence betrayed, but of the beautiful and devoted wife whose gracious ways and womanly gentleness and resistless beauty had been the crowning glory of his happier life, the sweetest solace of his misfortune, who had crossed the seas in his behalf, only to be repulsed in despair — he thought of her, and his last words were "POOR CARLOTTA!"

For this will Maximilian be remembered. Not for his royal blood, but for that touch of nature which makes the whole world kin. There is not in history any dying words of saint or hero which appeal more tenderly to the universal heart of man than these.

We do not mourn over Maximilian's death, for execution for state offenses does not necessarily imply any stain upon personal honor. His faults were those of birth and inheritance. His virtues, his bravery, his tenderness, were of that rare and noble quality which forever receive the worship of woman and the admiration of man.

"POOR CARLOTTA!" However misguided in his ambitions or his acts, those words, with their re-deeming associations, will crown him with the flowers of affection and the laurel of fame. This is one of the tragic facts of life, which eclipse all possible fiction. The romance of "Romeo and Juliet" does not equal in tearful and tender interest the story of Maximilian and Carlotta.

"POOR CARLOTTA!" The words are historic for-evermore. Side by side the brave young prince and his beautiful wife will walk together, grandly but mournfully, through the pages of future history — through all the years of coming time.

MINNEHAHA is *not* a "big thing," though it is one of the most curious and delightfully charming things on record. The water falls because it can't help it. The stream being small, and venturing to the edge of the precipice, of course the force of gravitation takes it down. It is natural, very. It flows music-ally along, like any other modest and merry stream, until, without warning of any kind, it suddenly finds itself on the dizzy brink, and in an even sheet about thirty-five or forty feet in width, it goes shivering and sparkling over, and shimmers and gurgles and gleams, and tosses out its white arms, and flings its silvery spray, and wreaths itself into fantastic forms, until, at last, having fallen, probably, about eighty feet, it gathers itself together and hurries away.

THE TYPE AND THE TYPOS.

The two most fascinating sounds, not human, to which I have ever listened, are the click of the telegraph and the click of the types. There is a tie of consanguinity between these sounds — a family relationship of birth, and a similarity of service in the things themselves. Each serves the highest master — Mind; each is engaged in the noblest occupation — the diffusion of ideas and intelligence.

As the music of the violin is an incentive to dancing, so is the music of types rapidly falling into a "stick" an aid to thought. Many very brilliant newspaper articles have been "set up" at the "case," without having been previously written, and in our experience we have often found that when we had an extra amount of writing to do, we could do it more easily and more rapidly to leave the carpeted sanctum and the cushioned chair, and sit at a bare table in the "composing room," where we could catch the infection of the industry around us.

Of the types themselves we never weary. They are the civilizers — a dictionary reduced to its lowest denomination. They look dull enough, but all the glorious possibilities that the human heart can hope for are in their possession — you have but to learn the secret they so closely keep. If one but knew how to properly pick out and arrange those little pieces of metal, princely fortune and immortal fame would be his reward. It took but a handful to make the "Heathen Chinee," yet that handful made the name of Bret Harte a household word, and placed ducats at his disposal. There are plenty of possibilities left in them yet. There are finer strains there than poet has ever sung; there is keener wit, more tearful pathos, more persuasive prayer than tongue has uttered, or ear has heard. Get it out if you can. They are patient of delay.

It is interesting to trace the analogy between these types and the mind which is their master. A locked "form" gives no more indication to the unpracticed eye of the satire that may be sparkling, or the sorrow that may be sobbing through it, than an impassive face gives of the thought which may be moving in the brain. And again, as the life of a man is often quickened, his soul strengthened, and his energy increased by stress of adverse circumstances, so it is only a "tight squeeze" which reveals the life within the types. The baptism of ink must descend upon them, and the strong arms of the press must embrace them before the life that is in them is made manifest.

The "typos" are as interesting as the types. The printer has been well called "the adjutant of thought." He is more than a mechanic, although much of his labor is mechanical. The faithful, conscientious, pains-taking printer is deserving of an honor that he rarely receives. Quite often he is the superior in intelligence of the writer whose "copy" comes into his hands, and it is owing to his judgment and care that the writer makes so presentable an appearance in print. Standing silently at his case, busy with hand

and brain, the "copy" that comes to him is a minia-
ture panorama of the multitudinous life of the world.
A jest, a murder, a speech, a song, a funeral, or a
dance, each is chronicled and forgotten, just as they
are briefly commented on and forgotten by the busy
world outside.

Among "typos" there is a fellowship closer than
among any other artisans. To belong to the "craft"
is a passport to the sympathy of all. The needy
printer can always find a "case" which his more
favored brother typo will relinquish to him for a
time, or he will receive a donation by asking for it.
No printer, whether deserving or not, goes empty-
handed from the office where his needs are known.
These needy printers are frequently the veriest "dead
beats" in existence. As the faithful, careful printer
is one of the most honorable of the great army
which swells the ranks of labor, so the "tramp" is
one of the most useless and degraded of loafers. In
being this, he but obeys a general law—that law
which makes a vile woman viler than a man can be,
because she stoops from a higher elevation. But we
have not time to pursue the subject. To all the
toilers at the case we reach out a friendly hand, and
hope that when their life "proofs" are revised by the
Master's eye, there will be found no "outs" of virtue
or "doublets" of vice.

THE way a man spends Sunday is a pretty good
indication of how he will spend the remainder of
the week.

5

THE COUNTY FAIR. — A County Fair, like death, or politics, is a great leveler. All meet on equal terms — the dapper gent and the hard-handed son of toil, the elegant lady and her humbler country cousin, the fastidious and the vulgar, the man of bowels and the man of brains, the white-haired and aged infirm and the red-cheeked, rollicking boys, all meet on a level and wonder at the pumpkins and admire the pictures; praise the address of the speaker and the trappings of the fancy team; are delighted with the music of the band, and eloquent over the enormous proportions of a yearling calf; applaud the graceful carriage of the lady equestrian, and linger admiringly around the pen of a beautiful Suffolk shoat, now talk interjections, with wondrous exclamation points between, as they examine a delicate sample of embroidery, and then almost affectionately caress a huge melon, a blood beet, or a jar of plum jam. And then when the fair is over, and the roads leading countryward are filled with returning teams, each load throws out talk as a fountain jets out spray, and for a day or two following the whole country is sown thick with gossip growing out of incidents connected with THE FAIR.

A TROUT is an embodied poem — the expression of God's finest thought of beauty of form, grace of motion and elegance of attire.

PROGRESS moves forward by two springs — men and events.

WINTER.

Winter is an institution — especially in this north-
ern climate. It comes late in the fall, and stays till
the weather is so warm it can't very well stay any
longer. This year it has come like an attack of the
rheumatics, or a caller before breakfast — mighty
sudden and unexpected. The smile of the Indian
Summer had scarcely faded from the hillsides, when
the surly wintry wind came blustering over them,
and made the bare treetops creak with pain, and
dashed a snow-shower all over the garments of retreating autumn. It was no sportive frolic of the
elements, but a genuine blast from the Winter King
—"a nipping and an eager air" that stung the
mouth which breathed it; while the mercury, which
for months had been reposing at figures of comfortable elevation, suddenly betook itself to the basement of its tubular tenement, and ran down to an
alarmingly low figure below nothing.

And now, my friend who holds this paper, (you
are not in much of a hurry, are you?) supposing we
have a little talk about winter. Cold is a very solemn
thing. It is cruel, remorseless — there is death in
its touch. We have got to battle for life till summer
suns shine on us again. Did you ever think of it—
that this Jack Frost, who paints your windows with
such delicate tracery, who clothes the whole landscape with jewelry which gleams and flashes in the
morning sun — that this same sparkling fellow is

more cruel and unrelenting, more pitiless than any ghoul or demon, or giant Bluebeard who affrighted your infancy? Perhaps you are a mother, holding your little babe full of rich and vigorous life. Divest it of its warm garments and place it under the clear sky of this beautiful night, and Jack Frost will sting it with icy pains till the soul is tortured out of the body and the warm child is frozen clay. And then, who knows but the wintry forces may increase, and the air become so full of frost that to breathe it shall be death, and furs and fires shall be of no avail, and we all be frozen stiff and stark, standing in the streets — sitting in the houses — motionless, dead; who knows?

Winter, too, takes away many of our pleasures. We will instance but one — the pleasure of going to bed when weary and rising when refreshed. A contemplative and philosophical mind can find but few pleasures equal to that of going to bed in the summer season. What a kindness in the touch of the delicious evening air! What a sense of roominess in the spacious bed! What a glorious chance for the legs to push round and get acquainted with each other! In the daytime a fellow's legs, cased up in cloth and boot-tops, are kept in perfect isolation and know scarcely anything of each other; but at night they are introduced to each other, and learn that they are fellow-pilgrims, traveling through life together. And in the morning what a luxury to get up! You can dress at your ease, and bathe if you wish, with no disagreeable chills running over you, but a sweet sense of secure and untroubled comfort.

But in the winter — ugh! You hang around the stove long after you ought to go to bed, and finally start off feeling that you have a disagreeable duty to perform. You undress with frantic energy — a shudder — a desperate plunge —.a spasm — a series of smaller convulsions — and you go to sleep just to dodge a feeling of discomfort. In the morning it is the same struggle over again. The thought of getting up brings a contortion to your face, and when impelled to it by necessity, or the thought of coffee for breakfast, you push yourself out with a sullen desperation, draw on a few indispensable articles, and rush for the nearest stove in indecent haste and in almost immodest attire.

For an unseen, impalpable thing, cold is about as certain a reality as there is in existence. It coffins up the lively streams, chills the bosom of the blossoming earth, and raises the price of cord wood. It puts a glow of health, a flush of beauty and rushing blood, upon the cheek of the delicate maiden wrapped in furs; and a look that is almost like agony — a wan, thin, pinched, despairing look — upon the faces of the shivering, tattered, and comfortless poor.

No art can elude this keen searcher. It nestles in the corners of the cheeriest room, as twilight lingers all the summer day in the thick boughs of a dark old pine. The roaring fire drives it back for a time, but, let the glow subside, and it comes back and chills to death the very embers. It pinches everybody's ears — nestles in the daintiest slipper, and crawls into the stoutest boot. No mortal power

can vanquish it, and only when the vast forces of
Nature give it battle, and the summer suns pour on
the world their flood of warmth, does it relinquish
its grasp; and then it is not conquered, only baffled,
and retreats to its strongholds in the icy North, leaving pickets in shady and sequestered places, and soon
sweeps down on us again, impalpable as a thought,
and dowered with a strength of which thought cannot conceive.

Yet let us not be too hard upon this rough old
winter. His hoary locks and glistening beard entitle .
him to a thought of kindness yet. Nature is full of
wise and beneficent compensations, and winter gives
us much for what is taken away. The long, quiet,
cozy evenings, when the fire burns brightly, and the
shadows dance upon the wall, and the fresh papers
are on the table, and the leaves of the new book or
magazine are waiting to be cut, and the sense of
discomfort without gives added blessing to the sense
of security within — what hours are these for thought,
for reading, for happy social converse! How the
heart grows, and is filled with a kinder love and a
holier humanity! With what resistless eloquence
come the pleading voices of the suffering poor, the
sorrow-stricken, the unfortunate!

THERE is a thread in our thought as there is
a pulse in our heart; he who can hold the one
knows how to think; and he who can move the
other, knows how to feel.

DEATH OF WEDDED LOVE.

We have all seen the trees die in the summer time. But the tree, with its whispering leaves and swinging limbs, its greenness, its umbrage, where shadows lie hidden all the day, does not die all at once. First a dimness creeps over its brightness, next a leaf here and there sickens and pales, then a whole bough feels the palseying touch of coming death, and finally the feeble signs of sickly life, visible here and there, all disappear, and the dead trunk holds out its stripped, stark limbs, a melancholy ruin. Just so does wedded love sometimes die. Wedded love, girdled by the blessing of friends, hallowed by the sanction of God, rosy with present joys, and radiant with future hopes — it dies not all at once. A hasty word casts a shadow upon it, and the shadow darkens with the sharp reply. A little thoughtlessness misconstrued, a little unintentional neglect deemed real, a little word misinterpreted — through such small avenues the devil of discord gains admittance to the heart, and then welcomes in all his infernal progeny.

The presence of something malicious is felt, but not acknowledged; love becomes reticent, confidence is chilled, and noiselessly but surely the work of separation goes on, until the twain are left as isolated as the pyramids — nothing left of the union but its legal form — the dead trunk of the tree whose branches once tossed in the bright sunlight, and whose sheltering leaves trembled with the music of singing birds.

A GOOD "TAVERN." — The —— tavern itself is a 'big thing." Whether viewed from the office, bar, billiard-room, parlors, dining-hall or chambers, it is somewhat stupendous. The ceilings are lofty — likewise the bill for a week's board, extras included. As a candidate for the nomination for circuit judge of this district once said of the City Hotel at Hudson, "the rooms are carpeted, and you don't have to come down stairs to wash."

A daily paper is published by the ——, called the "Bill of Fare." There are two editions — morning and noon. It is furnished to guests gratuitously, and is distributed by newsboys — who are girls mainly. Many choice selections are made from this paper. Much more might be said in praise of this tavern, but time faileth us. It is an excellent place to be in.

BOOKS. — A good book is the most appropriate gift that friendship can make. It never changes, it never grows unfashionable or old. It is soured by no neglect, is jealous of no rival, but always its clean, clear pages are ready to amuse, interest or instruct. The voice that speaks the thought may change or grow still forever, the heart that prompted the kindly and cheering word may grow cold and forgetful, but the page that mirrors it is changeless, faithful, immortal. The Book that records the incarnation of Divine Love is God's best gift to man, and the books which are filled with kindly thought and generous sympathy are the best gifts of friend to friend.

THE NEW YEAR.

Many of our readers are the same to whom we have sent greeting so many times before. Many of those early readers are now past all earthly hearing, and the same types which conveyed them greeting have recorded their departure.

Could we but write their real lives to-day — the history of their hearts — could we but catch and imprison in words the impalpable life of the soul — the happy fancies and the delicious dreams which tantalized them with the vague hope of something better than they had known, remote but longed for possibilities which drift through the dreaming thought as fleecy cloudlets drift through the far-off summer heaven; or could we picture the sorrow, the regret, the disappointment, the unrest that embitter life, or the black remorse that darkens it like a dream of hell; could we but thus picture even the commonest life, the passion of romance would pale in the presence of the more passionate reality. But the journalist deals only with outward facts and symbols, and real life remains unwritten and generally unknown.

The thought that some of those around us who now look out upon this glorious earth, and drink in its life-giving airs, and feed upon its beauty, will, on another New Year, lie buried in its bosom, is a natural thought. It intrudes itself upon us, and will not be put away, for it is true. The richness and

fullness of life as surely suggest the coming stillness
and darkness, as the shadows are sure to nestle
among the leaves in the rich heart of the summer
day.   The spectre confronts us not alone in the
closet, but he walks beside us in the brightest day,
and intrudes upon our happiest moments.

GENIUS AND POVERTY. — It is one of the mysteries of our life that genius, that noblest gift of God
to man is nourished by poverty.   Its greatest works
have been achieved by the sorrowing ones of the
world in tears and despair.   Not in the brilliant
saloon, furnished with every comfort and elegance;
not in the library, well fitted, softly carpeted, and
looking out upon a smooth green lawn, or a broad
expanse of scenery; not in ease and competence, is
genius born and nurtured — but more frequently in
adversity and destitution, amidst the harassing cares
of a straitened household, in bare and fireless garrets, with the noise of squalid children, in the midst
of the turbulence of domestic contentions, and in
the deep gloom of uncheered despair, is genius
born and reared.   This is its birthplace, and in
scenes like these, unpropitious, repulsive, wretched,
have men labored, studied and trained themselves,
until they have at last emanated out of the gloom
of that obscurity the shining lights of their times —
become the companions of kings, the guides and
teachers of their kind — and exercised an influence
upon the thought of the world amounting to a spe-
cies of intellectual legislation.

GETTING WELL.

Sickness brings a share of blessing with it. What stores of human love and sympathy it reveals. What constant affectionate care is ours. What kindly greetings from friends and associates. This very loosening of our hold on life calls out such wealth of human sympathy, that life seems richer than before. Then it teaches us humility. Our absence is scarcely noticed or felt. From the noisy, wrestling world without, we are separated as completely as if the moss were on our tombstones, yet our place is filled, and all moves on without us; so we learn that when at last we shall sink forever beneath the waves of the sea of life, there will be but a ripple, and the current will move steadily on. On a sick-bed the sober truth comes home with startling emphasis, that

> "The gay will laugh
> When thou art gone, the solemn brood of care
> Plod on, and each one as before will chase
> His favorite phantom."

But we started to write about getting well. There is a luxury in getting well that cannot be told. To feel that the links binding you to life are surely strengthening; to be a little stronger in the feet; to take the first unassisted step; to be an hour longer from the pillow; to sit once more with the family circle; to venture into the open air and feel the

better for it — yet all the while to be a little tremu-
lous with fear : this is getting well. It is to the
frame something as spring is to reviving nature —
when we are not quite sure it has done snowing;
not sure but a narrow breadth of winter — a " re-
lapse," you know — lies between us and the full
blossoming violet and snowdrop.   One feels a new
life tingling in his veins, and it seems as if this
wondrous machinery of his was just set in motion.
The faces of acquaintances, too, wear a strange
look, and only by degrees do they grow familiar.

But a weakness in the arm, a trembling of the
hand, and a dizziness of the brain, warn us to close
this article, lest the fatigue of writing interfere with
our own — getting well.

THE TOILET OF DEATH. — The love of dress is
instinctive.   With the child it is a passion, with the
woman a pleasure, with the man a manly pride.   It
is necessary and right to give due attention to our
apparel, and bestow befitting care upon our personal
appearance.

But the time will come when we shall not make
our own choice of clothing — our own hands will not
arrange it, nor our eyes take note of its appearance.
The child will take no delight in the beauty which
adorns the body; the woman will not perceive the
texture, color, or arrangement of her garments, and
the man's closed eyes will take no heed of his comely
apparel.   It is when the toilet of death shall be made.

ROBERT BURNS.

Probably around no other name, not divine, has poesy twined so many wreaths; over no other has oratory pronounced so many and so graceful eulogies; about no other does love cling with such tenacious hold, as about and around the name of Robert Burns. Scotland was his birthplace, but the heart of the world is his home.

If one wants to know how royal is song — how every gift and power dwarfs in its kingly presence, let him ken Robert Burns. He has lifted a provincial dialect into universal knowledge and interpretation. He has made the wild Scottish heather a house-plant, blooming by every fireside where literature finds welcome or love itself a home. Who knows who was king when Robert Burns was an exciseman? Who knows who were the lords, and the chancellors, and the generals, and the admirals, when he was treading in the furrow of his plow and watching the daisy curl beneath it? Who knows of their birthdays? Who forgets his? What he touched, of his age, will be immortal. Tam O'Shanter's hold on remembrance is as secure as Cæsar's or Napoleon's. "Highland Mary" will be enshrined forever in the world's heart as the true ideal of a maiden — gentle, loving and pure,— as sweetly, but less sadly, than Ophelia, she will glide through all the centuries to come — a vision of beauty, grace and love.

Burns, the smart plowman from Ayreshire, the rhymster, who excited after a while the mild curiosity of the *literateurs* of his time, dined one day, by sort of special favor, at Lord Munboddo's, with Dr. Blair, Dugald Stewart, Henry McKenzie and the rest. They came into the presence of the wonderful rustic thoughtlessly enough, and now they cannot return if they would. They are defrauded of oblivion, and must forever attend him as satellites the sun, or courtiers the king.

His very follies endear him to us, for we know how sincerely, sorrowfully repentant he was. He does not shine upon us with spotless splendor, in awful isolation, but walks our daily ways, shares our common thoughts, enters our open homes, loves, hopes, prays, sins and suffers like us all. If his follies were conspicuous, his nature was large. Small souls need small restraints. A man may carry a few drops of water in a pint cup on a smooth path safely, but to bear a brimming bucket over mountain ways, through storm and night, and never spill one drop, is what no man, not even Burns, could do. From his life, as well as from his lines, we learn the great lesson that

> " We partly may compute what's done,
> But know not what's resisted."

All over the world his birthdays are celebrated, and his name kept in loving remembrance, but no florid eulogy or stately verse will pay him a finer tribute or more truthfully delineate his crowning excellency, than Alice Cary has done years ago, in words simple as his own :

> " A lover of the beautiful,
>   In Nature's sweet evangels ;
> For his great heart was worshipful
>   For men, and maids, and angels."

THERE are trees, like the butternut, which impoverish the ground upon which they grow, but the olive tree enriches the very soil upon which it feeds. So there are natures as unlike in effect as these — some cold, selfish and absorbing, which chill and impoverish every one with whom they come in contact. Others, radiant, affluent souls, who enrich life by their very presence, whose smiles are full of blessing, and whose touch has balm and healing in it, like the touch of Him of Nazareth. Squalid poverty is not so pitiable and barren as the selfish heart, while wealth has no largess like that with which God dowers the broad and sunny soul. Be like the olive from whose kindly boughs blessing and benison descends.

TO-DAY there is no scholastic seclusion so profound that the allied voice and action of this mighty living age may not perpetually penetrate it. To-day the workshop has become *clairvoyant*. The plow and the loom are in magnetic communication with the loftiest social centres. The last results of the most exquisite culture of the world in all its departments, are within reach of the lowest haunt, where latent genius and refinement await their summons.

INFLUENCE is to man what flavor is to fruit, or fragrance to a flower. It does not develop strength or determine character, but it is the measure of his interior richness and worth, and as the blossom cannot tell what becomes of the odor which is wafted away from it by every wind, so no man knows the limit of that influence which constantly and imperceptibly escapes from his daily life, and goes out far beyond his conscious knowledge or remotest thought. There are noxious weeds and fragrance-laden flowers in the world of mind as in that of matter. Truly blessed are they who walk the way of life as the Saviour of mankind once walked our earth, filling all the airs about them with the aroma which is so subtilly distilled from kindly deeds, helpful words and unselfish lives.

ENJOYING RELIGION. — We are tired of hearing people tell about enjoying religion, or mourning because they do not enjoy religion. Religion was not intended to be enjoyed. Theoretically, it is abstract truth, like Euclid's propositions; practically, it is merely correct living. The object of religion is not to be enjoyed, but to enable people to enjoy life, and arm them with faith to meet that which lies beyond. It is a means, not an end; and people who are longing after enjoyment of religion are very apt to divorce it from its proper influence in mellowing the asperities of life, and prompting to kindness, charity and love.

NATURE is a creditor who accepts no protest.

VENTRILOQUISM.

[A local notice from the Prescott " Journal " in 1867.]

Professor Sands gave semi-scientific, magical and diabolical entertainments here on Tuesday and Wednesday evenings last. He had full audiences, and entertained them well. Some of his tricks were performed with a skill we never saw equaled. But the sharpest and best trick he performed was in inducing nineteen or twenty-three fools, one of whom was us, to pay one dollar each to learn how to perform ten tricks of magic and ventriloquism. We learned them; oh, yes. They were easy, and when we had learned how, we could perform them so easy — just as easy as a boy who has taken one lesson on a violin can play like Ole Bull, or a girl, after her first dancing lesson, move like Fanny Elsler.

But we learned ventriloquism good. It sometimes troubling us to talk where we are, we wanted to know how to talk where we ain't. We can do it. We can "throw our voice" muchly. We have tried it thusly: We are the proprietor of a bovine cow. She don't seem to know her master's crib as well as the Biblical ass did his. She isn't disposed to be regular to her meals and milking. This eccentricity was sometimes annoying. It is so no more. We step to the door and ventriloquise her. We throw our voice a mile or so to her favorite haunts and

6

win her home. We would not take ten cents for this useful and wonderful power of ventriloquism. We will impart it to our friends for a reasonable remuneration. We like Professor Sands, and hope he will rent a house and come here to live.

THE practice of asceticism in religious matters is, happily, fast passing away. The dogma — so commonly accepted even a few years ago — that self-denial is a thing commendable in itself and for its own sake; that the mere fact that an emotion or a practice is pleasing, affords sufficient proof that it is sinful and should be repressed, is one of the few remaining shreds of the now tattered robe in which superstition once clothed the radiant form of religion itself. We cannot inject virtue into the soul by drawing the blood from the veins. It is from the regulation of desire, not from its crucifixion, that virtue grows strong; · and warm-blooded, large-hearted, strong-passioned men and women, who guide aright the current of their lives, but do not check its strong impetuous flow, are fitter creatures for the uses of life and the service of God, than the pale, passionless human plants out of whom a too rigid discipline has crushed the bloom of earth without infusing the hues of heaven.

THERE are men so penurious that if an angel should visit them and stay to dinner, the cost of the meal would detract from the warmth of the welcome.

A FAMILIAR EPISTLE.

Now, Joe, I am taking it easy in shirt sleeves and slippers, with a cozy fire and a few capital cigars, and this letter will be a sort of random, helter-skelter concern, written a good deal as a pig makes a forced journey—in all directions—and so I direct it to you individually, that its semi-personal character may nick off the wire-edge of any unkindly criticism.

You are indebted for this epistle, dear Joe, to a tremendous snow-storm which has been howling around here until it is liable to indictment as a public nuisance. And I may as well remark that during my stay in this State snow-storms have been disgustingly common. There is an old saying that snow is the poor man's fertilizer—at least that is what it means, though the word used in the proverb is suggestive of a ranker odor and a more filthy appearance than we ascribe to the cleanly snow. Admitting the proverb to be true, it grieves me to think how much of this fertilizer has been wasted here this season. Millions of bushels have drifted away into uncultured places, simply because the farmers were too shiftless to build fences high enough to contain it.

[NOTE.—Will professed agriculturists please call attention to this fearful waste of a productive agency?]

Did you ever think, my dear Joe, what a powerful thing this snow is? You see the broad, feathery flakes, pure, soft and yielding, falling silently and slowly, touching the earth as tenderly and lovingly

as a mother kisses her child, and it seems a type of
harmless purity.   But by-and-by the snow-clouds
thicken and darken, the cold hardens the feathery
flakes into biting crystals, and the wind moans and
shrieks and roars like some fabled demon in an agony
of torture, while hour after hour the snow-shower falls
in a blinding tempest, and every living thing seeks
shelter from the fury of its rage.   And when the storm
is over, there it lies, massed into vast drifts against
which horses rear and plunge in vain, and the hissing locomotive, with its fiery strength, reaches into
it to retreat, baffled, beaten — and, not to put too
fine a point upon it, these huge snow-drifts keep
cattle away from drink, boys and girls away from
school, and men and women away from the neighbors, church, store and post-office.

[NOTE. — Right here, Joe, I may as well note the
fact that the most harmless appearing things have
the largest share of latent power and fury in them.
The fleecy cloud in the summer heaven looks so far
off, intangible and pure, that we might fancy it the
mere exhalation of a passing angel, but the lightning,
which touches but to wither, lies in its bosom.   It is
not the man "bearded like a pard," rough and blustering, whom it is dangerous to offend, but the quiet
fellow who utters no threat, gives no premonition of
anger, except the changing light in the eye, where
fixed resolve is burning.   .And then we all know,
either by observation or testimony, that the mildest-
mannered, purring, pussy-cat kind of women are the
most fearful when on the "rampage."]

But, to come back to the railway train: what a thing of mystery and beauty and power is the engine itself — I mean one of those ponderous, royal fellows, whose driving wheels move with consciousness of almost limitless power, and the arm which connects them plays as if it felt omnipotence was in its stroke. It is more marvelous than the human brain in one respect, for labor does not wear away its vital force. The play of those steel arms is tireless, and its onward rush never falters from fatigue. And then, how kind and tractable a monster it is! At the will of its master, it will repose in perfect quiet while the gentle lady alights from the car, and then, at a touch or too, it flames and shrieks, and rushes over dizzy heights and through gaping gorges as if hell was in its heart, and it was fleeing from mad avengers. Did you ever think, Joe, while riding in a rail-car, that you were as much at the mercy of the engineer as if he held a loaded rifle to your breast? Let him but touch here and there, and your trip would be a "through" one, for you would fly past the station where death stands ever, passing from one world to another. I sometimes compare an engine to the human brain. The working of a large brain, guided by wisdom and principle, is beneficent, like the power of a locomotive, when rightly controlled; but an essentially bad man with brain power is as dangerous as an engine fired and running with no directing hand.

By the way, Joe, I think it is not long since you were back from the State of your adoption to the

State of your nativity, as I now am. How much
seems strange, Joe, dwindled, as if we were viewing
things through the small end of a telescope. The
old stone schoolhouse, where I learned to "speak,"
and "compose," seems to have "run into the ground"
several feet. The church, with which is connected
my earliest remembrance of sermons and sabbath-
schools, and which seemed so vast an edifice to my
wondering youth, is now a very modest-sized and
rather mean-looking building, while the steeple, which
rose to so dizzy a height, is not now so lofty by far, and
it is leaning sadly askew, as if the devil were tugging
to pull it down, that it might no longer point the
way to heaven. And then those distances across
the flats, from house to house, or hill to hill — is it
the longer reaches we have traveled over since
which makes seem so short now what was such a
weary length in the years agone? And when we
meet local great men, whose riches or beetling brows
awed our boyhood, how we find our wonder and timidity gone. How *old* it makes one feel to ferret out
his *quondam* schoolmates, and find them filling re-
sponsible stations, grappling with life's earnest work,
and see lovely women who have gone into life-com-
panionship with them, and find the little diamond
types of humanity —

> " Feeble promises of future men "—

lying around loose most anywhere. But there is
another thing, dear Joe, which makes your correspondent feel older than all this — it is to meet some

one whom you remember as a pretty little girl in pantalets and short dresses, to whom you used to give candy and primers when you were a young man, and be *introduced* to her, and be received with an easy lady-like grace, and find yourself in the presence of beauty and culture, quoting Tennyson, and talking about "Great Expectations," and you invite her to a ride, a concert or a party. Ah! Joe, this makes one feel *very* old indeed — he looks for gray hairs, and wonders if he is not becoming venerable.

But, Joe, let us change the subject before it gets too solemn.

This being the 4th of March, I am reminded that for just one year Mr. Lincoln has been President of the *Un-tied* States. Let us hope that before the next anniversary of his inauguration, we may transfer the letters to their original place, and call him President of the *United* States.

You may have heard of an affair down in Tennessee, where a movement was set on *Foote* which resulted in giving an extensive land *Grant* to the rebels in the vicinity of Fort Donelson. There was Western blood and brain and muscle there, Joe. You have read, perhaps, of the rejoicings with which the news was received — the shouting, the display of banners, and the thunder of the guns. Somehow, Joe, I could not halloo much. I kept thinking of the thousands of poor fellows who were lying stark and stiff — severed by canon ball, riddled by rifle shot, torn by bursting shell, and trampled under foot in the deadly charge. Lying there, grimmed with powder and besmeared with blood, their ears are forever deaf to the exulting shout of victory. Of course the cause is worth the sacrifice, but I can rejoice better by-and-by, when the wounded have recovered, and time has partially soothed the sorrow for the dead. You have read, Joe, of that company which went into battle nearly a hundred strong, out of which but seven came back unscathed. No doubt they were mainly good fellows — generous, hopeful, strong — loving life as you and I do, and they had mothers, wives, sisters, and many, perhaps,

> "A nearer one
> Still, and a dearer one
> Yet, than all other."

And they shall welcome their coming no more! How will the days seem darkened to them, and life be burdened with the weight of an almost crushing sorrow! It is easy for us, safe at home, to talk of duty and honor and glory and liberty and law and the flag, and its being "sweet to die for one's country;" but still the shock of battle may well blanch the cheek and sadden the heart of the thinking and compassionate. The hearts which bleed are not those alone which are pierced by remorseless bayonet or murderous ball. They are scattered in humble homes all over a continent, and the wound is no less painful because unseen.

No MAN ever professed to contemn women until he was conscious of their contempt.

RELIGIOUS PROFESSORS.

There have been several instances, recently, in which clergymen deflected from the strict line of manly and ministerial propriety, and each instance has been seized upon by the rapacious reporters of sensation sheets, and magnified into an importance totally disproportionate to the offense. We do not so much care for this as for the covert sneers at religion itself which are introduced into these arti- cles — the inference drawn that because of these transgressions the Christian religion is impotent and powerless to restrain the passions and purify the life.

This habit of judging a cause by the exceptional case of one of its professed followers is not confined to reporters alone, but it is unjust, illogical and ab- surd. It is also true that people generally expect too great results to follow from a public profession of a Christian faith and practice. They demand of every "member of the church" a uniform piety and an equally blameless life. Now, in the nature of things, this expectation cannot be realized. Religion is simply a certain power — a moral force — and its effect upon any person is limited, and determined to a great extent by the character of the person upon whom it acts. To the man or woman of genial and sunny spirit, of frank and generous and noble nature, religion adds a grace almost divine in its unmatched beauty; but upon the man or woman with a natu- rally sour and cynical disposition, with coarse, uncomfortable manners and perverted instincts, the same power of religion acts only as a restraint— mitigating what else were altogether unlovely into a condition of comparative tolerableness. If you apply an equal amount of sugar to a dish of strawberries and a plate of salad, the taste of the two will not be similar, and so the same influence of the Christian religion applied to totally dissimilar characters cannot produce similar results. If one is not a professing Christian, let him at least be reasonable in his criticisms of those who are.

OUR lives are complex. Coöperation is the necessity of our being. It is the first lesson taught us — for no person was ever born without the presence and coöperation of another person of maturer years — and in the important and intensely personal matter of marriage, the coöperation and consent of another person of the opposite sex is absolutely essential. The thread of life, even with the most self-reliant, is not a single, separate strand, but it is twined and interwoven with many others. Numberless and unknown hands are laboring to supply our wants or minister to our pleasures. The Celestials pick the tea whose fragrance we sip, and laughing girls beyond the sea gather the grapes whose rich blood shall sparkle in the light of our homes. Not till we reach the close of life shall we be beyond the need, as beyond the reach, of human sympathy and aid. In that supreme, momentous moment, we are — for the first time in our existence — ALONE.

DEC. 2, 1859.

[The following lines were written the day John Brown was hung, Dec. 2, 1859.]

There's a sadness stealing o'er us, there's a hush in all the
    air ;
There are eyes grown red with weeping, there are strong
    hearts bowed in prayer;
And the patriot's cheek is burning with the crimson blush
    of shame,
While the whole broad land is thrilling to the mention of
    ONE NAME.

Old John Brown swings from the gallows — so Christ hung
    upon the tree —
Freedom's noblest son is strangled in the proud " land of the
    free."
But the cross is shrined in holy hearts and worshiped by the
    good ;
So the gibbet shall be glorious with sacrificial blood.

O brothers! are we dying? Have our souls put out their
    fires ?
Have we hearts of men within us? Have we Freedom's large
    desires?
Shall we sneak into our closets, and mumble out our prayers,
While a hero's dying gasp is burdening all the airs?

Dare we stand in glorious sunlight, and look up to God's pure
    heaven,
And no stern, indignant protest from our deepest souls be
    given ?

Let us wake from idle dreaming — wake from all unworthy
    care!
Fill our hearts with manly purpose — match our *action* to our
    prayer!

Let us think of John Brown's swinging from the gallows into
    heaven;
Till a portion of his manhood to our puny souls be given —
Till the holy fires of liberty our frigid hearts shall swell —
Till we hate this damned oppression with the bitter hate of
    hell.

But a glorious morn shall break upon the night of our de-
    spair;
Justice will not sleep forever, nor God be deaf to prayer;
Angels rolled away the stone where Christ glorified did lay,
And the sepulchre of slavery shall be luminous with day.

And when dawns that glorious future, and we've wiped away
    our shame,
John Brown, despite his errors, shall wear an honored name;
And eloquence shall warm its speech, and poesies shall play
Round the soldier-guarded gibbet, where the old man dies
    to-day.

AN IDEAL POEM.

A poem should be round and perfect as a star,
    And full of beauty, with truth beaming;
No vicious thought or ugly phrase should mar —
    But, like spring flowers in meadows gleaming,
It should shine out in brightness and in splendor,
    And be as holy, pure and fair,
As full of light and love, and tender
    As a fair girl's eyes, or a saint's sweet prayer.

CHICAGO.

[Extracts from a letter to the St. Paul "Pioneer."]

I like Chicago. Chicago is a large city. I have noticed there are always many people in a large city. A city don't do well without them. Some of your readers may not have been to Chicago. Shall I tell them about it?

There are many groceries here, where they sell tea, codfish, whisky, flour, molasses, saleratus and such things, and other groceries where they sell cloth, women's clothes, and fancy feminine "fixins" generally. Field, Leiter & Co. have of the latter. It is in cube form — a block long, a block high, and a block thick. It is bigger than a barn, and tall as a light-house. There are more than forty clerks in it — some of the male persuasion, and some of the female sex — and every one of them is as slick as a spit-curl on the side of a school-marm's face.

There are shows here — theatres, where girls, without very much clothes on, will whirl around till a fellow is dizzy looking at them; and then stand on one leg, like a hen. Then all the fellows clap their hands, and the girl, she does the same thing again. It is fun; but I don't think I would like to marry one of them girls that jumps about as handy as a flea, would you, Mr. Editor? I don't think they would be real careful mothers-in-law, do you? Miss Olive Logan insinuates, you know, that—well — that they, that is, some of them, might be mothers out of law, but this may be because she couldn't get used to standing on one toe as long as they do. Jealousy prompts cruel words sometimes. Then there is a good show — Wood's museum — where there are birds, monkeys, wax-works and the moral drama. There is to be seen the dead skeleton of a big snake that aint alive now. The snake is a whopper, or was when he was on earth. It takes two to look him all over, one to begin at each end and look till they meet. He is as long as a board fence. A crow-bar would be just a fair sized tooth-pick for him, and he could put you in his ear and not feel it. I am glad he is dead.

There are lots of ships here, and horse-cars, but the horses don't ride on them, though, and the water-works. I must tell you about the water-works. They are a big thing. Much water is used in Chicago. Fastidious people sometimes wash in it. Chicago has first-class water now, and plenty of it. She has built a tunnel two miles long, and tapped Lake Michigan that distance from the shore. The water runs down to the home station, and is then lifted up high by steam-engines and distributed over the city. The hoisting of it up is a good deal like work. There are three steam-engines, of 400,000 horse-power each, used in' pumping up the water, and they are now preparing to put in a new large one. I like to see those engines work. Anybody would. Clean, polished, shining monsters, they seem to take a conscious pride in their performance, and the tireless movement of their mighty arms seems almost as resistless as the will of God. But they cost scrips, these piles of polished machinery and throbbing life do; and with that regard for economy which has always characterized me, I think I have discovered a plan by which this work can be done at a nearly nominal expense. I only wonder that Chicago, with her accredited "git" and "gumption," has not adopted my plan before. I will explain privately to you. My plan is this: At the shore end of the tunnel build a large tank or reservoir, put two first-class whales in it, and *let them spout the water up.* Simple, isn't it? and feasible, too, and cheap. You see the whales would furnish their own clothes and lodging, and all the oil they would need for lights to work nights by, and the city would really be out nothing but their board. Whales have always been in the water elevating business, so this would be right in their line. They would work and think it was fun — just as a boy sometimes, but not most always, does — and there is no good reason why their sportive instinct should not be turned to practical use. Their willingness to do a fellow a good turn is proven by the fact that several years ago one of them gave a preacher man named Jonah cabin passage for a three days' trip, and never even asked to punch his ticket at meal time, and didn't charge him half fare, but treated him like a first-class dead-head, and wouldn't take a cent.

I am confident of the final success of my plan,

but the prejudice of people against innovations may retard its operation for some time yet.

Speaking of water makes me think that Chicago, like St. Paul, has a river, only not so much so. Rivers most always run by large cities; they seem to like to, some way. But this is a brigandish sort of river, black, foul and murky, and in the dark night it steals sullenly through the city, like a prowling fiend. Sometimes drunken men stumble into it, and awake from their stupor in another world; and sometimes fair and beautiful girls, whose lives have been clouded with sin, and upon whom the intolerable burden of remorse and despair presses with a crushing weight, seeks its dark depths as a refuge — bury their griefs and shame — let us hope their sin also — in its bosom, and so, shudderingly, pass from the scorn and cruelty of life into the presence of infinite pity and boundless love.

There is a Board of Trade here, made up of merchant men and bliffers. Sometimes they sell what they haven't got, and don't have money enough to get it, and then their occupation is gone almost immediately. And there are meeting-houses — lots of them. Country people call them churches, but preaching rinks is the fashionable name. Some of these rinks are big and splendid, and people that go in them worship in a highly elegant manner. The music is better than in Brignoli's recent operas here, and the preacher men pitch into each other sometimes, and their "mills" are reported by the enterprising local papers here.

There are taverns here, no end of them hardly, and some of the quiet looking fellows that keep the books can beat Sheridan on a charge.

But I can't finish this letter. It is too hot. The mercury is clear up in the attic of its tubular tenement. I have "peeled" successive garments, till I should blush to meet a marble goddess, and so, sweating, but serene, I remain, yours truly.

THANKSGIVING — 1862.

Great Father of all tribes of men!
　Thou Sovereign over all
To thee our willing knees we bend,
　Before thee gladly fall.

We give thee thanks, O Sovereign King,
　For blessings from thy hand;
, O may thy presence light our way,
　Thy smile illume our land.

Though war's mailed hand is red with blood,
　And earth groans with the slain,
From seeming ill shall spring the good,
　Nor life be lost in vain.

For where our starry banner waves
　Our armies fight for thee;
And though the path lead over graves,
　The goal is LIBERTY.

7

THERE is no grace more becoming a man, no attribute more essential to the perfect development of his manhood, than *humanity*. Religion may add dignity to the lustre of this endowment, and reckless living may do much to mar its beauty; but this jewel, whether set in the fitting accompaniment of blameless living, or gleaming out from a disordered life, like virgin gold amid worthless dirt, still has an intrinsic worth which adorns and enriches its possessor.

By humanity we do not mean alone that natural impulse of the heart which prompts us to relieve physical want or suffering when presented to us, but also that more delicate sensibility which appreciates mental as well as physical conditions — that thoughtful and far-out-looking sympathy, which recognizes the suffering we do not see; that condition of mind in which its possessor, himself sitting securely in comfort and ease, still hears in undertones the weary cry of the world's suffering ones, and strives, not alone to relieve isolated cases of suffering, but to lift up classes and peoples into more hopeful and happy life. This is the true glory of man. Humanity like this, careful of small things, yet reaching towards large results, takes on the nobility of that *charity* which religion places first among the virtues, and the man who cherishes it in his heart has a royalty within him which he can no more hide than a prince can disguise his native bearing beneath the vestures of a clown.

SOCIAL CORRESPONDENCE.

Mr. Taylor had a very extensive social correspondence, embracing not only a large number of relatives, but a wide circle of other friends, most of whom were persons of literary tastes and habits, and among the number several who have won high distinction in the literary world. This volume furnishes space for only a few selections from Mr. Taylor's social correspondence, but these cover a long series of years, running from the school days of his early boyhood, nearly up to the time of his death.

The following are letters to a cousin. The first was written when he was but seventeen years of age, while he was at work in the stone quarries at Malone, N. Y. It bears date May 23, 1852 :

DEAR COUSIN :

No wonder Ik Marvel said, " blessed be letters." He didn't mean a short business scrawl, nor a freezingly polite and elegant one, prim as a young miss's new bonnet, without any sentiment or soul in it ; no, he meant a free, dashing, easy, chatty letter, full of trust, truthfulness and affection, one that was coined in the heart and not in the head ; in short, just such an one as I received from you two weeks ago.

Now, Mellie, are not such letters worth having? How much wider the world seems, how much better life seems, how the soul enlarges, and the affections deepen while reading letters that come fresh from the heart. * * * I am glad you were so well pleased with the poems I sent you. Thanks for the urgent invitation to make you a visit. I tell you, Mellie, I had planned a visit to you when I returned home, and thought much of the pleasure it would be, of the warm, hearty grasp of your hand, and, perhaps, give you a — a—k— (excuse me, Mellie, no use in dodging) a kiss, and receive a much better one, besides seeing the other whole house full of cousins.   But the return of our folks from the west changes all my plans, and now I cannot tell when I shall see you.

You say you have read "Dream Life."   Wasn't it a treat, though?   I believe that " Dream Life " will do more good in the world than all the sermons of many Christian preachers who have grown gray in their sacred office.

Now, Mellie, write soon ; I cannot afford to wear out my boots running to the office in vain.   Good bye.

Your aff. Cousin,   LUTE

MIDDLEBURY, May 29th, '53.

DEAR COUSIN MELLIE:

Here I am, in the good town of Middlebury ; its gray old college staring me in the face ; the famed "green mountains " rear themselves around me, their proud tops half hidden by the light mist which, driven from the valleys, clings around their summits, as if reluctant to float on heavenward ; the rich fields are smiling in the sunlight, and the bob-o-link is trilling his song as merrily as if there was no such thing as heart desolation in the world.   You will probably wonder at my dating from M., but the "thread of true love " is not the only one that does not run straight and smooth, and we are continually reminded,

> " There's a Divinity that shapes our ends,
>   Rough-hew them how we will."

School closed three weeks ago last Friday.   Mrs. W. was taken sick.   Last Sabbath they discovered that her lungs were diseased.   Monday counsel was called, and pronounced her case very·critical.   Monday night she failed very fast, and Tuesday, about twelve o'clock, she died.   She was perfectly aware of her condition, and talked freely and calmly about it. Her death was easy and peaceful — just as the taper burns to the socket — flickers — expires. The death-bed scene was very impressive to me. When they saw that she was sinking, I called in the minister and a few neighbors. When we entered the room she was lost to consciousness — had already entered the dim, mysterious realm, where the golden light of heaven meets and mingles with the dark shadows of earth. We knelt in prayer, and in a short, earnest petition, the man of God commended her to the Saviour, and prayed that her departing spirit might be received where there is "fullness of joy forevermore." Oh, Mellie, how are we taught the evanescence of all things earthly! How are we admonished that

> "Life is but shadows — save a promise given
> That lights the future with a fadeless ray,"

and when we see the earnest, the hopeful and the young dropping away from the dusty path of life, how fitting seems the blessed entreaty —

> "Come, touch the scepter — win a hope in heaven,
> Come, turn thy spirit from the world away."

Mrs. W. has always treated me with marked kindness, and I have been in her society so much for the last six months, and enjoyed it so well, that her death seems more like a dream than a reality. There are dark spots on the sun of life, Mellie, but let us pray for each other that we may so live that we may at last be received into that bright world where

> "Each tie
> Of pure affection shall be knit again."

I was very much pleased with your comparison of our characters, till you made the exception in my favor. Pooh, Mellie, you didn't mean to flatter me, I know, but you are a little mistaken as to my abilities. You know every neighbor-

hood, and almost every family, has some "wondrous child,"
who is to "bring the flown muses back to men." I suppose
I have been so unfortunate as to be deemed one of that class.
What I might do I know not, but I never have accomplished
anything, either in study or writing, above mediocrity. During the past six or eight months I have read a good deal of
our best English literature, and while I have enjoyed a great
deal of pleasure in reading it, I have been enabled to see
plainly my thrice diminished inferiority. I have lately been
into the prose works of Coleridge. They are a rich mine of
thought. One feels, on laying down the book, as if he had
been carried to some high eminence, where the soul breathed
in its native air. I never got at the wealth of Burns till
lately. His melodies flow as free and artless, as sweet and
charming, as the bird songs. My love for Willis "grows
with my growth." His earlier poems I like the best. There
is a tenderness — a delicacy — a fragrance — a truthfulness
about them which is truly bewitching. While they glitter
with beauty like a polished diamond, they are still the reposi-
tories of his true heart-life, and they will be read as long as
poesy is loved and admired.

The scenery around the mountains here is grand. The
breezes give one new life and vigor. I never enjoyed the
spring so much before. It seems as if I should love to give
myself up to its sweet influences ; " commune with Nature in
her visible forms," and learn lessons of gratitude and thanks-
giving to the great Author of all. What a beautiful figure
that is which represents heaven as an eternal spring !

Your coz.,   LUTE.

Under date of May 12, 1855, he writes, in refer-
ence to abandoning the idea of attending college, as
follows :

You say you wish to know my plans. My whole stock of
plans at present are these — to write a little, eat, and go to

bed. The idea of going to college I have pretty much given up. There are evils in life about as bad as ignorance, and one of these is to be everlastingly in debt — a calamity.which, with heaven's help, shall never overtake me. I have neither grace nor genius enough so that I could conscientiously receive aid from any benevolent society, and so the by-laws of my constitution seem to preclude my going to college. Longfellow, in " Hyperion," says, " The setting of a great hope is like the setting of the sun." But, you know, when the sun sets the stars come coyly out, and so I may find many quiet joys and wayside pleasures from which a college life would shut me out. But the sun of my hope has not wholly set, though its disc has dipped sadly below the horizon.

SABBATH, 5 O'CLOCK, P. M.

DEAR MELLIE:

I wish you were here this afternoon. It is not always we feel like visiting, but if you were here now I know we would have a quiet, pleasant and cousinly chat.

You made a little apology for writing in a spirit somewhat sad. No need of it, dear cousin. For myself, I never intend to fish with

" The fool's bait — melancholy,
For the gudgeon — opinion,"

but the cloud and the sunshine alternate in the summer heaven ; and so, sometimes, the clouds will dim the sunshine in the happiest heart. I do truly believe that sorrow is holier than joy, and tears lie nearer the heart than smiles. I know that the letters which I most carefully preserve and oftenest re-read are not those which sparkle with wit, but those which dim the eye and awaken serious thought. I like to receive letters from you, cousin, written in every mood of mind, because they give me the assurance that you have a *whole-hearted* sympathy with me, and, I trust, I have the same with you. To most of my correspondents I reveal only one phase of. character, but to you I write in all moods.

I frequently have such doubts and fears as you relate. I hardly know what to think of my spiritual state. I know I have a love to God for his goodness, yet I have little of the spirit of devotion. Faith often is weak, and painted visions of sin have a strange charm, and I feel a mysterious power tempting me to shake off all restraint and lead a life of wild and reckless freedom. The set phrases of theology appear to me dead and unmeaning. I have bothered my brain too much with metaphysical reasoning — with speculation on things "beyond the reaches of the soul." My belief in creeds is shaken, but I still hold firmly to the belief that the name of Christ is the only one given under heaven among men whereby we may be saved. This afternoon the minister took for his text, "Come unto me, ye that labor and are heavy laden, and I will give you rest." I looked for a description of the *felt* wants of the soul — of those yearnings for something higher and holier — of that strange unrest we often feel ; and then, I thought, the love of Christ and the rest of heaven would be shown in words of lyrical power and beauty which would lure the weary, wandering soul to Calvary, while the choir, I thought, would surely close with that sweet hymn of Moore's, "Come, ye disconsolate," etc. But the sermon was logical, and the music noisy and heartless, and I came away dissatisfied, but, perhaps, all the fault was with myself.

Ah, cousin, the way of life will sometimes look dark and uncertain, but we must walk forward with what faith we may have.

> "It may be that the gulfs will wash us down,
> It may be we shall reach the happy isles."

I have been reading "Bertha and Lilly ; or, the Parsonage at Beech Glen," by Mrs. Oakes Smith. The style is pure and musical; the thought fresh, strong and elevating. It is written in earnestness, and deals some strong blows at existing practices in social and religious life. There are a few things which I do not like, but, as a whole, I value it highly. It draws character in clear and vigorous lines ; it deals more with inner than with outward experiences, and is admirably fitted to awaken thought upon those things which most concern us as immortal beings. Bertha is a calm, intellectual; spiritual woman, with that divine intuition which sees truth however hidden, and the moral courage to

" Dare all things which she knows to be right."

She has a soul filled with poetry and passion, but she sits a queen over it, and its desires and loves are holy.

I send you a little scrap of rhyme, not because I value it much, or suppose you will, but friends are apt to be indulgent critics. It came without calling, one Sabbath evening, and so I took a pencil and jotted it down, just to treat it handsomely, as I would any guest. As I grow older I enjoy poetry with a keener relish, and, as I have a truer perception of what poetry is, I make fewer rhymes; indeed, I have done *making* poetry.   Your cousin,

LUTE.

MADRID, *Aug. 19th, '55.*

DEAR COUSIN MELLIE:

Will you never write to me again? Do the duties of life press so closely on you you can find no time to use the pen? Did you not know you promised, when you went away, to answer some of my letters? I believe, if I want to hear from my friends, I shall have to go to Oregon, or somewhere else. If you do not write before long, I will — come (or go, rather,) to Canton, to see what the matter is. To-day I felt a strange unrest. I was going to take Byron, and lose myself in the wild, rushing current of his verse; but I knew I was not in the right state of mind to go to him, so I overcame the temptation, and got a package of letters of yours and others, and, need I say, I spent a pleasant and profitable hour in their perusal. Dear L——! she seems dearer to me now than ever, for she has passed the Stygian stream, and entered the " bright city of our God." How true it is,

> " We know not of love's might
> Till death has robed, with soft and solemn light,
> The image we enshrine."

Her quiet and serene trust in the Heavenly Father while stepping from the shore of life into the wide, unknown future, has given me more of faith than could all the reasoning of theologians. I see her to-night as I did the morning when I last saw her in life. She sat in the rocking-chair during family devotion, and well I remember the expression of her countenance as she joined you in singing the hymn,

> " Father, whate'er of earthly bliss," *etc.*

As the hymn was being sung, I thought the petition for "a calm and thankful heart" was answered, and I have often since thought how surely did his presence " crown her journey's end." I have never since listened to that hymn but, in fancy, I have seen her pale, sweet face, and heard her low voice mingle in the strain. Do you, Mellie, feel *certain* that there is a better world — a heaven where loved ones *live* in very truth? At times I feel a full conviction this is so, but, again, doubts *will* come that there is any intelligent life beyond the tomb. I know better, but I have not faith enough to drive the devil away.

Is it unkind in me, Mellie, to call up to your mind thoughts that dim the eye and sadden the heart. If so, forgive me. But you will not think so. If the dead live, and we are to live with them, why not talk and think of them as we do of other friends separated from us. I believe one of the great joys of heaven will be the opportunity for friends to hold free and unrestrained communion with each other. To-night I have felt kind love for many friends, and longed to sit by their side, and quietly and pleasantly hold heart communion with them. But when we meet we shall be soiled with the sweat and dust of worldly life ; we shall chat about the insignificant things of the present, and thoughts that in quiet hours plead for utterance will be forgotten. How rare it is here on the earth that two kindred spirits meet in that high sphere of friendship, where, without restraint, the heart can speak of its hopes and fears, its wants and desires, its visions of beauty, its vague yearnings for the good unattained. But I must write no more now, lest I grow gloomy, and I am determined to cut the acquaintance of the blues. So good night, cousin, and God grant that

> " We may walk this world
> Yoked in all exercise of noble end,
> And go through those dark gates across the wild
> That no man knows."

Your cousin,

LUTE A. TAYLOR.

MADRID, SABBATH, P. M., *Aug. 26th, '55.*

MY DEAREST COUSIN:

Many thanks to you for your last letter. Oh, cousin, how such words of kindness, of confidence and trust lift the soul into a better atmosphere and make life more bearable! You ask, Mellie, that I will not think any the less of you for showing me some passages of your inner life. O no ; I feel assured that the better we understand each other, the broader will be our ground of sympathy. Forgive me, cousin, for my words of indifference at parting with you. I was sorry the moment the words had passed my lips. The thought of repelling any flattery on your part never entered my mind. Never, even in thought, have I accused you of flattery; though sometimes I have thought you overrated my abilities. I felt sad to see you drive away, for I felt that, probably, our paths in life would be widely separated, and that I might soon lose even your occasional companionship. I do not think I am very reserved or cold in language when with friends I love and trust, but I have an antipathy to expressing feeling before others, and so my words often give the lie to my thought. It may be a weakness, and I think it is, but you must set down to its account any unmeaning or indifferent words I may ever speak to you. I suppose, Mellie, if I was a philosopher, I should prove that as excessive joy is often shown by tears, and the most crushing grief finds vent in hollow laughter, so the truest and deepest love, despairing to truly interpret itself in affectionate speech, throws out light words of indiffer ence or jest.

But I must tell you some good news. I have got four new books: "Memoirs of Margaret Fuller Ossoli," in two volumes; her "Woman in the Nineteenth Century," and "The Blithedale Romance," by Hawthorne. Mother thought I was a little foolish to get them, but she does not understand my case. Books are a necessary adjunct of my life. I do not look upon the reading of books as the *end* of life, but as a *means* to enable one to understand the right end of life, and as helps to fulfill it. By nature I am not a thinker. The necessities of my being do not compel me into thought. Without the aid of books I should sink into an *animal*, and I feel that is a thing to be shunned. The past year, which I have spent at home, has been very pleasant and profitable for my heart, but my head has been a loser. A few fancies like the "Chamber Scene" have been almost its only tenants. The fact is, if one labors in the earth his thoughts will be earthy. Shakspeare is right where he says one's nature

> "Is subdued
> To what it works in, like the dyer's hand."

For this reason, I believe the farmer — the business man — has urgent need of those books which serve to quicken and keep alive the ethereal spirit within him. The memoirs of Margaret Fuller have done more for me than any other book I ever read, excepting, of course, the Book of God. She has taught me, more than any other, "to open the deeper fountains of the soul, to regard life here as the prophetic entrance to immortality, to develop the spirit towards perfection." I feel I am a slow learner, yet my reverence for the teacher is none the less. Were I a Catholic, she would be my chosen saint.

Sept. 2d.— I have been at home to-day with the children.
I have been reading most of the time, and it has been a calm
and blessed day. I suppose we ought to go to church; but,
after all, I do not think I get as much good as by staying at
home. Amid the waving of fans, the rustling of ribbons and
silks, the snoring of the sleepers, and the idle or satisfied
look of the men or women cased in Sunday clothes, my
thought does not so easily take hold of the high views of life
as when alone. We have been reading the "Blithedale Romance" evenings. When I first read this book it interested
and excited me the most, I think, of any book I ever read, and
my interest was but little diminished on the second reading.
I could see the thoughts took hold of L——, for his prayer
at evening worship had a clearer aim — a greater breadth and
earnestness. I judge of the activity of a person's inner life
much by their prayers. If there is new and rich experience
in the heart, it must give birth to new and meaning words.
But with the most who pray, does not one stereotyped form
of expression last them through life?

But, to return to Hawthorne. I believe he has a hearty
love for purity and truth, but his keen eye detects moral de-
formity, and with steady, unflinching hand, he lays it bare,
not in bitterness, but in sorrow. Sometimes he lays aside
the probe and pruning-knife, walks with us in the scenes of
nature, and indulges in pleasantry and humor. But I do not
think he will ever be read by the multitude. His works have
not enough of sensuousness in them. But he will be read by
the connoisseur of human passion, by the student of character, by those interested in a spiritual life, who will yet
follow out thoughts which may lead them to doubt things
they had been taught to believe.

I have such a cold I cannot spare my hand from my nose
long enough to write more.   Yours,

LUTE.

RIVER FALLS, WIS., *June 23d, 1860.*

DEAR COUSIN MELLIE:

Like Daniel Webster, you " still live." Well, Mellie, I am glad to hear it. I have a recollection of formerly corresponding with you — indeed, in hunting over my manuscript treasures, this afternoon, I saw a number of letters which I am positive were in your handwriting. I also think I have a recollection of seeing you some time in years gone by. I think I went with you once to the " hill country" called Pierrepont, one autumn day, and sat beside the grave of one who had formerly sat often with you ; and, returning, we stopped at a place, and I brought away a little case, (which lies in my secretary, within reach of me now,) which always reminds me of you.

But really, dear Mellie, I am glad you have written once more to me. I have been expecting to write to you for a long time, but have not done it. I write very few letters, except what my business compels me to, and I have nearly lost, if I ever had, the art of doing it. But I do not suppose you want a *nice* letter from me — a kind of Lute-letter will suit you better, I know. I supposed you were owing me a letter, but perhaps not.

Say, Mellie, what do you think of this world ? I have an idea that it is quite well adapted for the residence of just such persons as you and I. With strawberry shortcakes and good cigars, and a good, dear mother to keep me in clean linen and good advice, I feel very well reconciled to life.

I want to see you, Mellie, and become acquainted with you in the character of Mrs. and mother. What are you, Mellie ? A girl still? or a patient, thoughtful, woman? or a delightful combination of both? Probably Charlie would say the latter, but I would not give a five-cent paper of chewing-tobacco for his opinion on the subject. What do you think of Tom Moore's " Lalla Rookh " now? What of the novelists? What of all the rose-colored dreams of boys and girls, your own former achievements in that line included? Isn't marriage a terrible alchemist, at whose touch all these fair and fanciful combinations of things dreamed of and hoped for, crumble and lie charred and dead in the crucible? Understand, now, I believe in married folks loving — of course I do — but I want to know whether love warmed by Hymen's torch is like that kindled by Cupid. Is it a patient kind of Christian "putting up" with things? or is it the genuine "seventh heaven in a glance," tempest in a teapot, etc.? An early answer is desired.

But about that little, dear, diminutive edition of humanity, who doubtless makes you so much trouble and gives you so much joy — I am glad she has learned that I am "mamma's cousin.' Well, you give that little one a kiss for me, and don't (as I know you will be apt to) tell her that I am a great and good man, but tell her I am a jolly fellow, and like to play with the little girls, and tell them stories, and stand them on their heads, and give them primers and candies, and so on and so forth.

But I have to go away, and must stop. Please write soon, dear cousin, and believe me

Yours affectionately,

LUTE.

PRESCOTT, *June 1st, 1865.*

DEAR COUSIN MELLIE:

I suppose, Mellie, I am one of the happiest fellows in this world — in fact, I don't see why I should not be. The ambitions, the vague desires, the feverish unrest which boys of any spirit always feel, have quieted down, and I am just a happy, contented, jovial fellow.

I shall not startle the world any, if I can help it — and I am pretty sure I can. For my wife and I — I simply pray

"Touch us gently, gentle Time!
Let us float adown life's stream
Gently, as we sometimes float
In a quiet dream."

You, Mellie, would enjoy such a life, I know.   Work
enough, but of an agreeable kind; leisure, books, music,
friends, rest.   I believe you will be so fixed one of these days ;
but the trouble is, life is short, and is fast going.

Summer opens to-day with marvelous beauty.   It is the
day of mourning for the great man gone, and the almost
Sabbath stillness is broken only by the magnificent steamer
which is just rounding up to the levee.   A nation solemnly
mourns to-day and sets its seal of approbation on the official
life and private character of Abraham Lincoln.

> " A martyr to the cause of man !
>   His blood is Freedom's eucharist,
>   And in the world's great hero-list
> *His name shall lead the van.*"

How strange it is that many good men will be such fools.
To-day the scholars in all our public schools met together,
and there was singing, prayer, and talk about Abraham Lincoln.   The talk was almost all sheer nonsense and ridiculous
lies.   Abraham Lincoln was represented as a model boy, who
never swore, or played in the dirt, or cried for bread and
butter, or chewed tobacco, or licked another boy, or ran
away, or did anything else that boys like to do ; and the idea
was held out that every boy there might be President if he
would be like him.   How ridiculous ! Half those children
know that Andy Johnson was President, and that he and half
our other Presidents were drunk sometimes.   Such namby-
pamby talk does not deceive half the children even, and those
who do believe it now as they grow older will see that it was
all false — that it takes brain and work and power to win
position, and that immoral habits, unless exceedingly gross,
are no bar to high official standing.   Integrity, ability and
capacity are wanted to manage public affairs, and the skeptic
is as apt to have these as the churchman.

Then there were over one hundred little girls there, and a
good man and great fool talked to them — how when they
grew up to be young women they should never marry or have

anything to do with a young man who chewed tobacco, smoked cigars, played cards, or drank beer. Wasn't that silly? I should have been an old bachelor under that administration of affairs, surely. I do all these things, and yet my wife thinks and says I am the best husband in the world — and I believe her. Well, I didn't mean to rattle on this way — a model letter this will be. Yours always,

LUTE.

The following are extracts from letters to a young lady friend:

LA CROSSE, *Oct. 8th, 1872.*

MY DEAR M——:

Have you got entirely out of patience with me for neglecting to write you? Have you "admitted" (entirely to yourself) that Lute Taylor is not the gentleman you supposed him to be? Have you vowed, in silence, to let him go many weeks or months without another welcome letter from you?

Ah, my dear girl, if you have done all and several of these things, I pray you to reconsider. Your letters have been gladly welcomed and greatly enjoyed by me. I have thought of you perhaps more than a married man should think of an interesting and talented young lady. To all this, I am willing, Miss M——, to make oath before any notary public who has a seal, or any magistrate, officer or judge who is legally qualified to receive solemn evidence.

Why, then, you indignantly ask, have you not written to me, when you knew I was among strangers and would highly prize a letter?

My dear girl, when will you learn to have patience, and not interrupt a person when he is making a statement? I fear you do not fully comprehend the great benevolence and self-abnegation of my nature. You know that there is no diviner act than forgiveness. It is exalting, ennobling. I am anxious to have you as noble as possible. You must have occasion to

8

forgive. It is education. You can now forgive me, and thus I will be an humble instrument in promoting your greatest good.

Oct. 17th. — Well, now, this is something of a recess, is it not? Broke off imperatively — then a few days' absence, a few days' sickness, the inexorable claims of business, the unavoidable claims of politics, and the numerous claims of social courtesy, and — well, here I am at 7 A. M., and nothing *mortal* can get audience of me until I have finished, enveloped, directed this letter, and placed it in the mailing-box.

When this confounded election excitement is over, you will find me a more reliable correspondent. This letter I don't count anything, for it does not amount to anything; but " by-and-by " I will atone for it, and until then believe me

Your friend,
LUTE A. TAYLOR.

LA CROSSE, *Sunday, Sept. 8th, 1872.*

MY DEAR FRIEND:

Your very welcome letter came Friday morning.

I have never read a letter from you with greater pleasure than this one. You were a trifle " blue," my glad-hearted, exuberant-spirited girl ; and do you know that when we have the "blues " we tell the truth, and we write only to those with whom the invisible ties of mutual liking and natural companionship are strong? And so your letter conferred a pleasure and conveyed a compliment.

Of course I know you have the " blues "— seasons of depression — occasionally. They are the penalty of intense spiritual life and rich intellectual endowment. The pendulum which swings high in one arc of the circle vibrates to as high an opposing place, and so high as the singing soul sits on the fancy-lighted mount of hope and joy, so low must it darkly descend into valleys of cruel doubt and almost shuddering despair. It is the law of compensation, you know The giddy girls of your rural neighborhood know nothing of the

fine ecstacy of your inspired hours, but neither is it possible
for them to feel the sharp pain, the exquisite agony which will
sometimes torture you in dumb hours of doubt and distrust.
Genius, power, breadth of vision, intensity of feeling, quick
and sensitive perception — these are glorious gifts, but they are
regal, and imperative also.   Such splendid guests cannot be
lightly entertained.   But if such life is not a boon, then anni-
hilation would be the goal of happiness.

Very truly your friend,

LUTE A. TAYLOR.

LA CROSSE, August 18th, 1872.

MY DEAR MISS M——:

Your pleasant letter, with photo. inclosed, came yesterday
morning, and, for once, I will not let procrastination steal
away the time for answering it.

I am glad that, in epistolary matters, you find it "more
blessed to give than to receive," and are willing to write me
six letters for one in return.   But, my dear girl, I shall not
allow you to do it.   No lady whom I like can have all the
talking to herself when I am around.   But I am glad you are
not exacting, and will not resent any apparent neglect on my
part.

Do you know that I am very glad that our brief personal
acquaintance is ripening into mutual friendship and esteem.
Knowledge is increased, experience enlarged, and life enriched
with every worthy new friend.   Men and women are the
flower of earthly life, and superior to all the attractions that
even affluent Nature can offer.   To learn one of these well is
more and better than to learn a new language or visit a
foreign clime.   And so, I prize my life as richer since you
have come within its horizon, and become one of the small
but cherished company who share its thought, encourage its
toil, and awaken its love.

Many thanks for the photo.   It is a charming picture, and
I think a good likeness.   I expected to ask you for one, but

had not, as I think I am probably the most timid and modest, if not bashful, gentleman of your acquaintance.

Do not work too hard, — do not let the fever of fancy burn up the rich blood of life. And you will not. Youth is prodigal of wealth; but coming days will inevitably teach you to carefully gather the harvest of thought, and only offer what is worthiest and best.

It is the bane of active newspaper writing that one has no time to improve; but you will never be connected with a paper so as to feel this tyrannous pressure.

But — good-bye for the present. Remember that, among all your friends, none feel more joy in your success, or more faith in your future, than   LUTE.

The following extracts are from letters to a former correspondent of Mr. Taylor's paper, who wrote over the signature of "Belle."

PRESCOTT, WIS., *April 27th, 1868.*
MY DEAR FRIEND MISS BELLE:

Have you about made up your mind that I was not intending to answer your two very welcome little letters? Well, that just shows how the best of women will be mistaken sometimes. Their intuitions, rapid as lightning, outrunning the processes of reasoning, are generally unerring as logic, but not always so.

I warrant, Miss Belle, that it never occurred to you that my long delay is the most convincing proof of the sincerity and strength of my friendship. But you will admit it now, I know. You know that if I should receive a pleasant note from a pleasant lady, of whose good opinion I was careless, that I should hasten to answer it. Courtesy, and every instinct of a gentleman, would prompt to this. But with a friend, you know— a real friend —whose confidence we hold by no uncertain tenure — how different it is! One does not have to be punctilious, — he presumes on the friendship, and shows the strength of his confidence by the amount of his presumption He sins with impunity, because he knows he is sure of forgiveness. You will thus see, friend Belle (what, come to reflect, you must have seen before), that my delay in writing has been only a delicate avowal of a feeling for you such as I would have if I had been lucky enough to have been your cousin, or, in some other way, been made sure of a permanent place in your kind remembrance. [Just here let me say it will not be necessary for you to acquaint me with your feelings in a similar manner.]

But again, Miss Belle, some way I have been terribly busy about nothing for several months, — away much of the time; and when I had time to write, it seemed as if my mind was too dull to write to you. You never have been a *business man*, have you? Well, don't be. It is terribly irksome much of the time. I came down to my office to-night to write business letters, but such employment seems like profaning the sweet, sacred beauty of the night. I was disgusted with it; and so I write to you, — a sort of grace before meal, — a placid morning prayer before the sharp struggles of the day.

But I must begin writing this letter. Let us be very proper, and commence on the conventional topic — the weather. Our Spring, making fair and early promise, has been very slow to fulfill her pledge. The bluffs are yet brown and bare, and the grass only just tinges the fields with its green. The robin has just come to-day, and the few early flowers "come in such questionable shape" that I have hardly dared to speak to them. You, I know, are in the full flowering of greenness and beauty, — Spring wearing for weeks the finest attire her wardrobe supplies. Yet I doubt if to-day your eyes have feasted on much greater beauty than mine. I watched the sunset, and the brilliant combinations and delicate shadings of color for a half-hour after, until I felt exhilarated and intoxicated with beauty, and the blood sprang warm to my cheek, as if the life and vigor of rare wine was in its flow. Lake and river were hushed, still, translucent, — a

thin, impalpable, glory-lit haze brooding over them, like a
gossamer veil on the face of a bride, — the heaven above
seeming to stoop to kiss the heaven below, save where the red
glory of the descending sun, reflected from low-lying clouds,
glowed on the waters in colors as rich as the purple stain
which a lover's clinging kiss leaves on the lips of his maid.

I just now think, Belle, of several things I would like to
write to you about; but those "business" letters must be
attended to.   Sincerely your friend,

LUTE A. TAYLOR.

P. S. — If you have not read Owen Meredith's " Lucille,"
do not lose an opportunity to do so. It is a pretty ripe
poem, — no " Leaves of Grass."   LUTE.

Under date of June 20, 1868, in speaking of
friends, he says of his mother:

Mother is quite smart, but yet I know she must be near-
ing the close of life; and she seems dearer to me as she
draws nearer to the "other shore." She will leave mourners
here, but she will find friends there.

LA CROSSE, WIS., July 20, 1869.

MY DEAR FRIEND BELLE:

What are you going to do about it — I mean about my
totally inexcusable neglect (as it seems to you) to write to
you? What have you done with me? Am I blotted out of
your book of remembrance — erased from your list of correspondents — totally non est — expunged — obliterated — gone?

Begging your pardon, Miss Belle, I don't believe any such
thing. When you have thought of my remissness at all, it
has been simply to regard it as a kind of mystery — like the
relation between free-will and fore-ordination, — something
that would come out all right, and be satisfactorily explained
sometime.

Now, let me explain the reasons of my delay.

1st. I delayed, without any reason, until I was ashamed of myself, and then I did not want to write until I could write a *good* letter, and I have waited in vain for that time, until I give it up.

2d. It is so pleasing to be forgiven by a pleasant lady friend — to say "*Peccavi*" and be absolved. You may forgive me, Miss Belle, — I assume that you will, and I feel better already.

3d. The practice of forgiveness is very wholesome. It is not only of itself one of the first-class virtues, but it strengthens and adorns all the others ; and, with a friendly care for the beauty and symmetry of your character, I have given you the opportunity to forgive me.

There! Am I reinstated now in your good graces, — placed again on the old footing of easy and informal companionship?——Thank you ; I thought you would excuse me.

You have read "Gates Ajar," of course. What do you think of it? I think it is remarkable — not a mere pleasing, ephemeral book ; but profound, logical, true. I believe that, as "Uncle Tom's Cabin" touched the national heart, awakened the national conscience, and gave a mighty impulse to that political action which has revolutionized the South, and blotted out slavery, — so will this book go far to awaken new and better trains of thought, and revolutionize the commonly-accepted ideas of heaven, — or, rather, give an idea where there was none before. I *believe* in its theories, — always have, — though I never gave my thought tangible shape, — never tried to reason on the matter, as this book does. I have often insisted, to the surprise and almost horror of the "Deacon Quirks," that, if I ever got to heaven, I should be an editor or reporter on the *Daily Celestial Sun.* I am sure of it now. I shall send the book to L——. She will enjoy and believe it. Do you know L—— is one of the best women in the world? The most valued compliment I ever had was that I was a good deal like her. Well, I think I am the same kind of a Christian that she is; but she is a great deal better one of the kind than I am.

Well, I must close. I think this is long enough for an apologetic letter. Very truly your friend,

LUTE A. TAYLOR.

LA CROSSE, *June 4th, 1871.*

MY DEAR FRIEND BELLE:

Now, that man who is with you need not take any umbrage at the possessive pronoun. You know it is used in a limited sense, but he can't rob me of any part of the small possession I have in you — not if I can help it. It might be as well to let him know this at the outset.

Your letter, Belle, brought me the first news that you had exchanged the Miss for the Mrs. — ceased an integral exist-ence and become a member of a firm. How did you think I would know it? I no more look at the marriage notices in the papers than you do at the calls for ward caucuses, or the quotations of Pacific Mail.

So, dear Belle, my congratulations come late, but heartfelt and sincere. Most heartily do I hope that reality may surpass expectation, and the promise of trustful love find full verifica-tion in the facts of daily life. I do not believe that your husband, or any man, is good enough to call you wife, though I certainly have a high regard for him from the fact that he is your husband. Honestly, Belle, don't you think that the highest compliment a woman can pay a man is to marry him? But I send you hearty greeting. You know what Tennyson says in the " Princess ":

" Not like to like, but like in difference,' *etc.*

Well, that is what I say to you.

Appointing you my proxy to introduce me to " Novy," as you so pleasantly introduced him to me in your delightful let-ters, and furthermore, and finally, warning you of displeasure, if not disaster, if in your new life you drop me from your list of correspondents, I am Yours affectionately, LUTE.

TWO PICTURES.

A few years ago, we were one of a party riding by stage from this city to Viroqua — a tedious journey at this season, at best — but its tedium was relieved by pleasant companions, and by the occasional magnificent stretches of scenery which almost rivals the Green Mountains of Vermont, or the unexcelled views which continually delight the eye about Harper's Ferry, and thence westward along the line of the Baltimore & Ohio railroad. When near our journey's close, a sight more pleasing than any we had met delighted our eyes.

We passed a party of comfortable appearing folk. Among them was a young woman, probably about twenty-five years of age. She was a brunette, with fresh complexion, dark hair and eyes, and held in her arms a babe which looked laughingly from beneath its protecting hood. But the mother seemed even more happy than the child. She appeared to hold up the beautiful babe as a challenge to all passers to share her joy and pride in its possession. We all noticed and commented upon this sweet spectacle of joyful mother and happy child. Of course, some pleasantry, or wit, or compliment from her companions might have brightened her features at that moment, but her look of sweet satisfaction and beaming pleasure seemed as if it dwelt there continually — as if the sacred joy and pride of maternity so filled her heart that it swam in light in her eyes, and rippled in smiles upon her face. It was a pleasant picture — more pleasant for being real — and each of us who witnessed it will cherish it as a "thing of beauty and a joy forever."

This is one picture.

The next morning we saw its counterpart. It was early when we started on our return. The vehicle itself — improvised for the occasion in place of the regular stage — was open and ill-supplied, with two narrow seats facing each other, without the remotest suggestion of comfort, coziness or warmth. The keen wind cut through our own abundant clothing, as we stopped to take in another passenger. She came. Great heavens! What an apparition of woe! It seemed as if direst poverty, utter ignorance and absolute lunacy combined could alone suffice to make a human being so utterly miserable and woebegone as she. A woman of forty or forty-five years of age, with heavy shoes, a worn calico dress, and evidently little under-clothing, a thin, miserable, cotton shawl, a light worsted hood — this was all her protection against the biting blast. Her hands were bare, and unkempt hair straggled over her sunken eyes and desolate face, which wore that mottled, lifeless hue which is the most touching evidence of extremest suffering and want. A few worthless rags in a coarse bag, tossed in after her, was her only baggage — no, not all, for here comes a little box; there is a smell of fresh paint on it, and it is of that shape and form that are never fashioned except to enclose the dead. We knew by the hungry look with which she devoured it that this was hers, and crowding it under the narrow seat, we went rattling away.

Of course it took but a short time to recover from our stupor of amazement, and, with the assistance of the kind-hearted driver, wrap her up in tolerable comfort. The straggling, almost incredulous smile of gratitude with which she received a pair of warm woolen gloves was something better to remember than the smile with which beauty receives her jewels, or wealth the luxuries which wealth can alone confer. The poor creature could speak but a few words of English, but we learned that she was entirely destitute of money, that she was traveling from Prairie du Chien to Buffalo county, and that on the preceding evening the child was taken from her arms, on the arrival of the stage at Viroqua, *dead*—dead without her knowledge of the fact. One needed not to be told that it had been dying since its birth, that inadequate food and clothing had combined to sap its little life, which finally yielded to the cold wind of a winter night, and somewhere on the dreary road, unnoticed and unknown, drifted out into the great unseen. Yesterday nestling close to her for warmth—to-day in the pine box under the seat. One can bear to look on the fine agony of a strong, sensitive, cultured nature, for the very strength which gives intensity to suffering will bring solace in due time; but here was wretchedness—weak, unreasoning, helpless and dumb.

And so we rode all the day, facing this picture of

want and despair and the little charity coffin. Looking at this, she would sometimes reach under her wrappings, and get out her worn soiled apron, and (with true womanly instinct turning it to the wrong side) wipe the half-frozen tears from her withered cheeks.

The luxury of tears, the divine sorrow of maternal love, was all that was left her. We could not help believing that the little one was better to-day than yesterday, better in the coffin than suffering and shivering in the mother's arms, but yet her grief could be assuaged by no such consolation as this. It might be that the only light of her life had gone out, that those thin wasted hands were the only ones that caressed her cheeks, those little pinched lips the only ones that touched hers in tenderness and love. Desolate! Desolate! In her seemed verified the full force of that pregnant passage of Scripture, "*without hope in the world.*"

And so the two pictures — happy mother and haggard wretch — smiling babe and coffined clay — sunny joy and shivering desolation — stand before us in startling antithesis, and, thus strangely mated, must remain in the close keeping of memory forever.

POEMS — whether in prose or verse — are simply open letters. No one ever writes a really good thing without, in thought at least, writing it *to somebody.*

IT is dreadful easy to be a fool — a man can be one and not know it.

FISHING, AND OTHER THINGS.

BEAR TRAP LAKE, POLK CO., WIS.,
June 12th, 1860.

DEAR JOURNAL:

Is there room for anything in print but wars and rumors of wars? Will matters of State and sensation dispatches, and wonder points, and military movements, and leaded leaders, make way for a garrulous article, drifting along over the paper, as aimless as a boat without steersman drifts before the capricious wind?

Sitting in this log cabin, looking out upon the water broken by the light wind into sparkling jets of silver upon the forest trees, with coloring so rich that they seem to sparkle with the light of intelligence, and swaying with a seemingly conscious nod, as if their matutinal salutations were not over; listening to the varied but not discordant bird-notes, coming like morning hymns from hundreds, yes thousands, of swelling throats; seeing no throng of· human life, hearing no hum of human labor; I can hardly realize that the great world without is awed into solemnity by the tragic events of the day — that all our own wide land is a drill ground for armies, and already loving hearts are sorrowing for the slain.

Looking at the baggy style of my clothing, its somewhat dirty and a good deal dilapidated condition; fishing down a long crane-necked bottle for

a little muddy ink, I can hardly believe that writing
is with me a business, and "copy" and "proof-
sheets" familiar terms.

You float over the placid lake, fringed with its
setting of dark pines, and its shallows rocking on
their surface the broad-leaved lily, with its almost
miraculous beauty, and it seems like the dawn of
creation, for the touch of time has not marred its
perfect beauty. You lie under the shadow of the
trees and listen to the puff of rivulets in the woods,
to the bird's note lessening in the languid air, to the
thousand sounds of varied life which fill the forest
with a low delicious murmur, and then a breeze
sweeps, like the motion of an unseen hand, through
the leafy greenness — the foliage shimmers and
lightly sways, and you feel

> "A divine
> Breath of the summer, full of coquetry,
> Happy and light and loving as a kiss
> Upon the eyelids from the woman you love."

FROGS.

But what have frogs to do with fishing? you ask.
A vast deal, my sapient friend. You might as well
try to have a wedding without a woman as to try to
catch a bass or pickerel without a frog — the thing
can't be done in any approved and decent fashion.

Now, many worthy people have an unworthy prejudice against frogs which should be dispelled. Being
as intimate with them as we have been, watching
eagerly for them by the side of ponds, holding them

tenderly in the hand, thrusting vest and trowsers pockets full of them, occasionally getting a small one mixed with the tobacco and smoking him in our meerschaum, we have come to a tender and loving appreciation of their excellence and merit. As dress is always a matter of interest, just look at the costume of the frog — a genuine hunter's, green as the grasses, scrupulously neat, and changing the whole suit two or three times a year.   Then what a voice they have!   What concerts they give by moonlight! Then, again, a "fellow-feeling makes us wondrous kind," and a frog is very like a man.   What a human leg he has!   How nearly its formation and appearance is like our own!   Then, who has not seen men with frog-like look — bald-pated, short-necked, puffy-cheeked and wide mouthed?   Such men are not apt to rule in political conventions, but they make excellent fathers-in-law.   Pardon us, reader, if we linger lovingly around the frog. As we have impaled him on our hook, we have taken lessons in the manly, heroic virtues. There is nothing sublime in the conduct of a young, dashing, frivolous fellow, who has never seen grief.   He squirms like a snake, and when you stick him on the bearded steel, he kicks like a devil and whines like a cross child ; but take an old russet chap, who has lived out eighteen of his twenty years, and braved the hardships of the wilderness, and incurred the responsibilities of the father of a numerous family : when you seize him, he gives a desperate struggle, and then resigns himself to inevitable fate. As the barbed hook passes

through him, not a moan of complaint, but a look
of heroic endurance and stoical resignation. But
enough of frogs; let us talk about

FISHING.

Your hook is nicely baited, the boat rocks gently
on the waters beside the sheltered shore, and you
are waiting for a bite. In the interval of expectation you descant on the lovely qualities of your frog,
and wonder that sensible fish can resist an induce-
ment so tempting. Soon you feel the snap of the
line and the tremor of the pole, and your strength
doubled by excitement; you tug till a row of black
spears shows above the water. Then how he struggles! careening on one broad side and then on the
other, till at last you bring him in "out of the wet."
A pretty good bass! About five pounds! Another
interval of suspense. By and by you feel a "symp-
tom;" — a moment of eager interest — it is a bite!
the line moves slowly against the wind — you know
your style, and, rising to your feet, give him line —
now you draw — gods! he is hooked! What a
moment of ecstacy! — how the supple, pliant pole
bends under the pressure! — now his white belly
gleams in the water as he comes slowly up — the
devil! — you have slackened line a little — the struggling fish has turned his head from you, and
whi-z-z-z-z-z goes your line around the bow of the
boat — you drop the pole and, seizing the line, draw
in, hand over hand, with eager speed — he is safely
hooked, and, cavernous mouth wide open, he comes

in out of the drink. You leisurely fix your bait, take a fresh chew of tobacco, ask the fellow next you if he saw how you did it, and toss out again.

AN INCIDENT.

A pleasing incident occurred one day which is worth narrating. As the bateau was drifting leisurely along, we discovered, on the opposite shore, a wannegan or punt, containing two ladies. Shade of Venus! Here was a schoolma'am! White dress and blue basque on Bear Trap! What an illustration of the aggressive power of common schools! The school house and the Indian camp within sight of each other! I never before so realized the picturesqueness of border life as when I saw the advancing pickets of education, with all its attendant amenities and arts, thus challenging the retreating sentinels of savage life. The position is one to be proud of. Boys, pass the glasses. Let us drink to the health of the maid on Bear Trap — to the peace of the schoolma'ams who basted us in our boyhood — to the success of the common school — to the glory of American institutions generally!

DEWDROPS come in silence and in the night. We sometimes think they are tears which the watching angels in pity shed over human sorrow or sin.

FUN is cousin to Common Sense. They live pleasantly together, and none but fools try to divorce them.

9

A HUMAN RUIN.

Any ruin is sad; a human ruin is saddest of all.
Whoever or whatever struggles for life and sinks
down battling bravely until engulfed by utter ruin,
moves our profoundest sympathy. The plant,
scorched beyond endurance by summer heats and
slowly yielding up its feeble life, touches our sympathy as if it were a sentient thing. The foundered
ship, struggling in tumultuous billows or breaking
against rocky shores, whose staunch timbers and
strong planks maintain to the last the ineffectual
struggle with wind and wave, seems to us to be ani-
mated by a human spirit, and its destruction calls
out a sorrow as if it were a human being, with love
of life and strength of will. The consumptive person, in whom the citadel of life has already been
taken by insidious disease, and whose strong will
matches itself against death, and resolutely scorns
to own defeat, though fading color tells of fading
strength, calls out a sympathy painful in its intensity
— a sympathy intensified by our yearning desire to
aid the sufferer in the unequal struggle, and our
utter inability to give effectual help.

Such wreck of health — such ruin of womanly
beauty or manly strength — moves us to grief and
saddens us with tears; but deeper, darker, more pro-
foundly miserable and utterly desolate is the spectacle of a strong man yielding to the mastery of drink
— the gradual loss of self-respect, the decay of the

moral sentiments, the growing paralysis of the will; until at last, utterly indifferent or defiantly reckless, he staggers through the dark door of death, with disgrace behind him and retribution before.

Not with one wild leap does any man go down this fearful abyss of sin and shame. The end is reached only after innumerable resolutions have been made and broken. It is a retreat in which the victim makes many a brave effort to withstand the demon who is pushing him on, and when at last disarmed of noble purpose, without the will to resist, or the ability to comprehend his disgrace, he sinks into utter and irremediable sottishness, and drifts almost unconsciously to his doom, it is the saddest sight in the whole universe of God.

A POEM.

[Extract from a poem read at a festival of the Franklin Club, River Falls, Wisconsin, in 1858.]

The soul that lives must daily grow;
Like Noah's dove, its thoughts will go
Out wandering, intent to know.

We live to learn — we live to glean
Some truth from every shifting scene,
And Winter's snow, and Summer's green,

And play of light, and song of birds,
And waving grain, and feeding herds,
And sweetest melodies of words,

And girlhood's laughter, ringing clear,
And sorrow's sob and pity's tear,
And dead friends — cold upon the bier, —

All things that soul or sense has caught,
With meanings rich and deep are fraught,
And furnish food for constant thought.

We open books, by use grown dear,
And the long centuries disappear,
As the far Past seems pressing near.

The beauteous queens of high romance,
Turn on us their impassioned glance,
And leave us in a willing trance.

The martyrs, sages, heroes old,
Whom love of truth or fame made bold,
Gleam on us from sepulchral mold;

And poets of the bygone days
Seem ever rising from their graves
To charm us with melodious lays.

*   *   *   *   *   *   *   *

Then give us truth that shuns no light,
While thought and toil their power unite
To clothe the soul with conquering might.

Thus, wisely living, day by day,
Our minds shall broaden, and our fancies may
Have wider scope and freer play.

Take hold of Nature's perfect plan,
And rightly estimate and scan
The life-work of an earnest man.

And, rising from this earthly sod,
Tread the bright path by sages trod,
Whose goal is only found in God.

A DISCURSIVE EPISTLE.

[Extracts from a letter to Frank Daggett.]

INDIANAPOLIS, IND., *July 7, 1868.*

MY DEAR BOY:

How does your robust form feel generally, with the thermometer indicating 98 degrees in the shade? Are you playful and happy as usual, or does the exuberance of life which generally distils from your speech and pen now exude at every pore, and leave you as uninteresting as common mortals? An early answer is requested.

But, seriously, the weather is very warm. I enjoy a continual bath in the perspiration of my own body, the only annoyance being that linen must be changed each twenty minutes in order to present a comely appearance. Now, twenty minutes is hardly long enough for a chambermaid to do the work of a room, and the maid who has charge of room 104, Bates House, in this goodly prairie city, is no exception to the rule. I have interrupted her while pursuing her ordinary avocations, and, when reprimanded, have boldly told her that a dry shirt I would have in spite of all the chambermaids in the house. If she had not been a charitable girl, and my face had not been a displayed advertisement of honest intentions, I fear I should have been reported at the office and persuaded to leave the house before the train left which I am going on.

But, to be serious, Frank, how *do* thin fellows get along this weather? You and I have generous frames through which to distribute the heat, and a broad surface from which to pass it off—but those thin, hatchet-faced, narrow-chested, slim-bodied, light-legged fellows, why, they must feel like a coal in a blacksmith's forge, like a bit of burned steak, or a muffin overdone.

How did you spend "The Fourth," my boy? I was in Chicago, and made up my mind that that city is more patriotic than pious. Never on a Sunday have I seen it so completely deserted as on the afternoon of the Fourth. The business houses were closed, the streets were empty and still, the people trying to keep cool indoors, or away in God's green temples—the shadowy groves.

But in the evening the streets were thronged with people in holiday attire, and the night glowed and shone and sparkled with all manner of fireworks, from the great lurid fires glowing fearfully against the sky, to the solitary rocket, which, speeding like a bullet, into the darkness above, falls back wasted —like a human soul which, having plumed its wing to mount to heaven and search out the mysteries of the *Infinite*, returns weary, baffled, and worn from its fruitless toil. I could not persuade myself to go inside the heated walls of the theater, and so I wandered idly about the city, viewing its splendor and its squalor, its wealth and its want—past the marble temples of trade—past the palatial residences of the rich, past the cozy, comfortable homes, out into

the suburbs — where in hot, close, crowded, festering tenement houses, women and little children
breathe an air that is poison and live a life that is
death — where gaunt poverty and grim despair form
a fellowship of misery, and from their loathsome
union is born crime, with its glaring visage and heart
of hell.

Give me the mountain and the prairie, the river and
the wood, the voice of passing winds, the sight of
growing things, the scent of flowers and the song of
birds — give me God's green earth, for I like it better
than the places man has built. I believe a life which
brings one into daily contact with the substratum of
a city populace tends to make him a materialist —
learns him to look at people as only another form of
animals, who live their brief life, perform their little
labor, and pass into the nothingness from which they
came. Philosophy and religion teach that a single
soul, an isolated human life, is priceless, outweighing
in value all material wealth; and yet, when we look
at the ignorant, unthinking, vicious, degraded and
damnable mob which swells the census of the cities,
it is almost impossible to believe that the Son of God
died for such, that gems of value are hidden in such
worthless caskets, or that a future better than the
present can ever dawn upon them. Yet it will not do
to cast away faith in the loving paternity of God.

> " How would it make the weight and wonder less
>   If, lifted from immortal shoulders down,
> The world were cast on seas of emptiness,
>   'Mid realms without a crown."

I am a serious lad, my boy, and, riding much on the cars lately, I have thought how much the trip on a train is like the journey of life. The incoming passengers, who burst in upon us at the way-stations, are the births which keep full the stream of life; while those who depart are quickly lost to sight and thought, as we shall be when we step off into the darkness which envelops all the world. The engine represents the human passions, which are the motive power of life; the engineer is law, which guides and controls; the brakemen are the magistrates and officers who watch over and protect our persons and property, and the conductor is the parson, who directs us on the journey and acquaints us with our destination. To finish the similitude, many go wrong in life, and many go wrong on the train.

With almost unimagined speed the world rolls along its measured track among the stars. Soon our station will be reached. We shall step off into eternal silence, and invisible Charon will ferry us over the Stygian wave. There is no baggage-master on that craft, my boy. Our checks must be surrendered before our spirit feet shall tread its ghostly deck, and so do not encumber yourself on the journey with things that must be left behind at its close. Thus, like many another, covering my own deficiencies with a word of admonition to a friend, I am

Yours fraternally.

WILL and WORK are higher trumps than genius and luck, in the game of life.

FOURTH OF JULY ORATION.

[The following short extracts are from a Fourth of July oration delivered at Winona, Minnesota, in 1872.]

* * * It is a matter for congratulation that our fathers chose this particular season of the year for the enunciation of their Declaration of Independence. Longest days, midway between seed-time and harvest. On each side the months slope down. All the luxuriance, the superb and sensuous beauty of nature greets us now, and contributes to our rejoicing.

* * * We may as well understand the fact that the old-fashioned Fourth of July has passed away, never to return again. It belongs to history. It is as much a part of the past as the battle of Brandywine, or the surrender of Burgoyne. Twelve years ago there was an awe in the sight of a cannon, a glory in the waving of a flag or the beating of a drum, and a novelty in the appearance of a regiment in arms. There was a charm of remoteness about these things. They moved before us as the actors move in a play. Since then they have become sadly but proudly familiar. The gaudy show has been made a stern reality. The cannon have thundered the menace of death; the drums have beat the solemn death-march; the gay banners have been torn by hissing balls, and the brave regiments have swept in shattered columns over fields that were lost. We cannot now invest the Fourth of July with its ancient reverence. We have handled the sacred things until they have become common and familiar. The heroes of the Revolution do not loom so grandly before our mental vision, for we find their living peers and equals wherever we turn.

As the advent of the Christian dispensation broadened the old, local, Jewish Sabbath into a universal day of worship, recreation and rest, so has the logic of events broadened this Fourth of July, which at first commemorated only the successful revolt of a few colonies, into a festal day of freedom, and made the very words a menace to oppression and an inspiration and hope to the oppressed.

The Fourth of July is the Nation's birthday, and it has probably occurred to all of you that the importance of a birthday is greatly in proportion to the age of the individual. It is a great event when the babe has completed its first twelve months of existence. The youth who has not attained his majority, thinks the years creep along with snail-like pace, and looks forward to his birthdays with never-failing interest, but to the man immersed in business they pass by almost unheeded; while the dimmed vision of the aged hardly discovers them, as the crowded, shortened years flit by.

What the years are to the man the centuries are to the world, and we have not yet passed the first century mile-stone on the journey of national life. It is only by comparison that we can appreciate how young, as a nation, we are. Away to the north, on the banks of Lake St. Croix, lives a man* who is older than the Fourth of July. His step is still reasonably firm; the light from his eye still gleams out from beneath the thin lashes which shade it; his memory is still tenacious; his enjoyment of the society of friends is fresh and keen; yet he is ten years older than the Fourth of July — was born ten years before the Declaration of Independence was signed — ten years before " The Fourth" was taken out from among other days, glorified, and made forever memorable. This man voted for Washington for the Presidency, and, holding him by the hand, looking into his wrinkled face, listening to his voice, you feel how young this country is. Four generations like him would reach back and clasp hands with that first emigrant to the western world — Christopher Columbus.

I sometimes think we do not give sufficient honor to Columbus. It is true that he was spared many things which fall to the lot of later emigrants. He had to " declare his intention " to the natives, but he did not take out his naturalization papers; was not implored to go to caucuses, or join a campaign club; he never ran for office and was beat, nor hurrahed over favorable election returns, nor lost his money on an unsuccessful candidate, nor was on the finance committee of a Fourth of July celebration. But though spared all this, his honors do not match his merit.

Looking back at him through the misty years, he

---

* David Stiles, who died in 1873, at the age of 107.

seems to us more like one of the demigods of mythology than like an actual living man — a hero of
history.   The world has never witnessed a sublimer
spectacle, a grander pilgrimage, than that of this
wonderful man, this princely vagrant and royal
beggar, burdened with ideas too large for the world's
acceptance, wandering from court to court with his
visionary, ridiculous and absurd ideas of a new
world, and begging for the means to enable him to
find it, until at last a foolish queen gave him the
necessary aid, and, with a fearful and superstitious
crew, he started on the long voyage across the vacant ocean.   The vacant ocean!   Just think of it!
Now it is white with the sails of every craft, from
the shapely yacht to the stately ship, while the great
steamers, with clouds of smoke trailing like black
pennons in their rear, shoot from the shore of one
continent to the shore of another, as a weaver's
shuttle flies across his loom.   But then all was vacant; the sun rode out of the wide waste of waters,
swung over the broad arch of heaven, and dipped
again in the boundless blue, and looked upon no
living human thing.   The storms stirred the great
ocean into thunderous tumult, but no human ear
listened to the grand diapason of the sea; no eye
saw its climbing billows and yawning depths; no
heart shuddered at its threatening peril.   The sea-
birds skimmed its surface, the fishes sported in its
waters, the great tides rose and fell, the sunlight
slept upon its broad expanse; but all was vacant,
unused and unknown.

So, too, this great continent was a wilderness, ripening for future use, where human life was savage, and all which we deem desirable was unknown.

* * * But let the procession of years pass by until you come down within the memory of living men, and even this vast west was a solitude, unpeopled, save by wild beasts and men scarcely less wild than they. The rivers flowed unvexed by the fretting wheels of commerce. On the broad prairies the flowers bloomed and died, with none to note their beauty; and the luxuriant grasses ripened in summer airs, rotted and enriched a soil on which no harvest waved. The forest trees, untouched by deadly ax, grew old and died, and their successors lifted their mighty trunks in air, like towering columns of great cathedrals, and along their high, leaf-woven domes the soft winds rippled, in their verdurous arches the birds sang, and from their mossy floors flowers sent up their praise in perpetual fragrance and perfume.

Now, how changed! Man has laid his hand upon the mighty forces of nature and subjugated them to his will. Seeming impossibilities have been realized, and the most startling wonders are the every-day facts of our lives. Harvests ripen in the fields; villages cluster in the valleys; cities sit queen-like beside the lakes and rivers; mines give up their hoarded wealth; spindles turn, and shuttles leap, and hammers thunder in mills and manufactories; the steamers come and go; the rushing trains sweep across broad States, making far-sundered people

near and familiar; the lightning leaps responsive to
our touch, and becomes a swift, invisible messenger,
conveying our words with the rapidity of thought
itself; while, better than all, school-houses dot all
the land, and, from every hillside and in every
valley, church spires point to heaven. Distance is
annihilated, time is stayed, opportunities are enlarged. During the past year mail service has been
put by this government on 8,000 miles of newly
constructed railway, and nearly 12,000 miles have
been built.

But, great as have been the triumphs of labor and
the growth of material interests, greater still have
been the triumph of moral forces and the growth of
ideas. The ideas of the fathers of the Republic
have become living facts; their theories have crystallized into laws. Freedom no longer sits in sorrow,
weeping over the atrocities committed in her name,
but, throned in regal state, wielding the sceptre of
law and armed with the word of power, her will is
imperative and her dictum obeyed.

Everywhere progress has been made. Thought
has been quickened, aspirations elevated, philosophy
broadened, theology liberalized, and life enlarged.
We have to-day all the conditions of free and pros-
perous national life.

The question of moment to us is, how shall we
preserve these conditions for ourselves, and transmit
them to those who come after us? In schools is our
safety, is the almost universal response. I know the
great value of schools; I would multiply their num-

ber, improve their character, and increase their efficacy. Politically speaking, there is virtue in a spelling-book, and the multiplication table is a means of grace. Yet, we must remember, that educated villainy is more dangerous than honest ignorance. The men who plotted the last great treason against the country were men of learning, polished in the arts which schools impart, and armed with the strength which they give. Many of them had been wards of the nation, trained in her schools, and honored in her service, yet they basely stung the hand that had blessed them, and stabbed at the life of their benefactor.

More men fail from want of character than from want of intellect. It is the vices outside of law which are sapping our national life. Personal extravagance and love of show and effect drive thousands delirious with care. Licentiousness blasts the beauty of social life, and blights soul and body with the mildew of hell. Intemperance seizes its victims and drags them from comfort and respectability to poverty and the degradation of loaferdom, and then sends them groping through dark delirium to the doors of death.

We fear no foreign foe. Our danger is from ourselves. It lies in the evils I have pointed out; it lies even more in the multiplicity of offices and the mad ambition to hold them; it lies in that unhallowed avarice which uses official position for the purpose of personal gain; in the decay of that nice

sense of honor which fears the commission of wrong
more than its exposure.

*   *   *   *   *   *

I am free to confess that I devoutly believe there
is sufficient virtue in the country to insure a pros-
perous and healthy national life. I see a future
stretching out before us radiant with promise and
rich in every possible blessing. I believe God has
a great work for this nation to do; that here the
problem of government by the people is to be
wrought out, and that in his providence we are des-
tined to be a teacher and an exemplar to the nations
of the earth.

We, Mr. President, may not live to see the full
fruition of our hopes, but those who come after us
will find here a government strong in the affections
of the people — a land where freedom shall reign,
where law shall issue its unbought edicts, where
Justice shall hold her scales with steady hand, where
Honor shall lift her unstained brow; a land which
shall be the realization of the patriot's hope and the
Christian's prayer; a land where the flag shall be
the symbol of freedom, as the cross is the sign of
faith, and whose benign influences, flowing forth to
farthest limits, shall make the Fourth of July a
sacramental day to all peoples in all lands.

EPITAPHS are like circus bills — there is more in
the bill than is ever performed.

CHAMBER SCENE.

Slowly the darkness rolled away,
Folded back by the fingers of day,
As in sweet sleep the maiden lay.

The rarest beauty was her dower;
She slept, unconscious of its power,
As fair as Eve in her Eden bower.

The fringed lids were closed above
Dark hazel eyes, brimful of love,
Which might have moved Olympian Jove.

The pillows swelled on either side
Her rosy cheeks, as if to hide
Her beauty, but in vain they tried.

Her warm breath with her tresses played,
Which, all unkempt, around her strayed,
While one fair hand uncovered laid.

The snow-white coverlet rose and fell
Responsive to her bosom's swell,
And mimicked every motion well.

Now birds their morning music made—
'Mid light and song awoke the maid;
She rose, and robed herself, and prayed.

Then rising reverent from her knees,
Unclasped the shutters, and the breeze,
That sported with the flowers and trees,

Came coyly in and kissed the maid,
And lightly with those tresses played,
That hung so stilly while she prayed.

10

Oh, she did seem surpassing fair,
And every breath of morning air
Was hallowed by her whispered prayer.

Thank God that not in heaven alone
Are pure and loving spirits known!
E'en here they bow before his throne.

And many a wild and wayward one,
Who else in erring paths had run,
By such pure souls to heaven is won.

ALL'S RIGHT.

[Flagmen were stationed at every road crossing, and every half-mile,
showing the American flag — a signal that all was right. — *Extract from
an account of Lincoln's journey to Washington.*]

Look, where the faithful sentries stand,
  Beside the level bars,
Each bearing in his trusty hand
  Our banner's stripes and stars.

The nation's chief doth ride to-day,
  Her hope is passing there ;
And love encircles all the way
  With keen and watchful care.

As eager eyes run o'er the track,
  The stars gleam on the sight ;
Each signal star is flashing back
  The welcome, " All is right!"

" All's right!" where shine those sacred stars
  Our chieftain's safety's sure ;
And when his hand that banner bears,
  ALL'S RIGHT!"— *it is secure.*

WHAT I KNOW ABOUT STAM-MERING.

[From a letter to the Milwaukee "Sentinel."]

The success of Mr. Greeley, in writing a book on what he knows about farming, has emboldened me to write a newspaper article on what I know about stammering. I am confident that I am much better informed on my subject than Mr. Greeley upon his, for he has entirely failed in his efforts to raise dried apples from the seed, while I have never failed, when called upon, to stammer to the satisfaction of private friends or public assemblies. Sometimes it has re-quired extra exertion for me to fill the measure of expectation, and give as great an amount of English, disjointed in a different manner from that in which Webster or Worcester disjoints it, as was expected of me in a given time, yet I have never failed to meet a reasonable demand.

[N. B.—I will qualify that statement by admit-ting that, sometimes, at political meetings, when the Democrats called me out in preference to other Republicans, because they thought I would say less against them than anyone else, I have surprised them by dropping the customary repetition of my pronunciation, and made all the counts against them possible in the time given me.]

Stammering is an art which but comparatively few people possess. I am the more surprised at

this, because it can be acquired without interfering
with any regular business, and, usually, practice will .
make one perfect.   I have known young boys who
were very strong stammerers indeed, and young men,
who have been with me, by strict attention and using
all their spare time, have made very creditable progress, and in a few weeks compelled me to check
them, lest they should become my equals or supe-
riors in the art.

Its advantages may not be apparent at first, but
they will be admitted when attention is directed to
them.

First.— It gives one prominence, singularity, notoriety, or whatever name you choose to call it by,
and everyone likes to be prominent, separate and
distinct from his fellows.   Who does not remember
some stupid play-fellow of his boyhood who stammered, and who is remembered for that fact, and
that alone?   But for this he would have been rubbed
out of your memory, as a sum is rubbed off from
the blackboard; but now he sticks, as the gashes in
that board, cut by stony seams in the chalk, stick.
An unregenerate Democratic editor, heated by partisan 'prejudice, once said that stuttering gave me
all the little notoriety and small consequent influence
which I possessed.   I reflected upon the remark, and
was suprised to see how truthful it was, considering
the unreliable source from which it came.

Second.— Stammering excuses people from many
things.   When I was a schoolboy, and became hope-
lessly lost in the conjugation of the Greek verb

tupto, a severe contraction of the face, a judicious movement of the under jaw, and a sort of appealing look in the eyes, as if I knew but could not tell, would cause even the stern old professor to bend on me a look of sympathy and regret, and nod to the next to finish my exercise, so that, without knowing anything, especially about my text-books, I was always marked high on examination days.   This was a great advantage to me, and gave me that leisure for outdoor exercise which young students so much need.   In the autumn it also enabled me to make great progress in the study of pomology in the many orchards in the country adjacent, and fellow-students became fond of me, and loved to frequent my room.   It is a noble thing to have one's fellows fond of him.

In the spring of 1853 I was attending school in North Bridgewater, Mass.   Returning home from Abington on foot one afternoon, I met a man, who stopped me to inquire the way to the town from which I had just come.   The fellow stammered fearfully.   I began to laugh at first, then, divining his wish, started to give him the desired information, and began to stammer myself.

"D—n you, do-nt you m-m-moc-mock me."

"I ai-n't m-moc-mo-mocking you."

The oath was repeated, and his brawny fist was shook so close to my eyes that I could not see beyond it very well, and his face fairly flamed with rage.   He was a horny-handed delegate, a good deal larger than I was, and I resorted to diplomacy instead

of war. I finally convinced him of my integrity,
and we sat down by the roadside and had as comfortable a social time as Artemus Ward's mother
and Betsey Jane's mother used to have boiling soap
together.

In the summer of 1857 I was publishing the "Journal" at River Falls in this State, and then, and for
some years after, there was in that town a delegation
of as active and reliable stammerers as I have ever ·
known. There were five of us. First, there was
Wm. J. McMasters, then foreman of the " Journal,"
now one of the editors and proprietors of the Lake
City (Minn.) " Leader," and then, as now, one of
the purest, kindliest and best men whom I have ever
known. Mac did not seem to like to stammer.
There was an apologetic air about his performance,
as if asking pardon for annoying his hearers. Mac
was the best foreman I ever had, because it was
known that the editor stammered ; and whenever I
was away, and Mac was in charge, he could fill the
whole bill. Then there was Mr. D. H. Levings,
now resident there. I have known him from boyhood, and have no hesitation in vouching for him as
a " star " stammerer. In conversation he works
everything about his face but his voice, and does
everything but talk. He has a wonderful facility
of distorting his features while wrestling with words,
and is a perfect success as what the theatre people
call a "muggist." He looks mad when stammering,
but he is not. It is his way. Mr. Henry K. White
was also a very competent and steady stammerer.

He put less emotion into the business than the others, but he was more even and reliable, and could always be depended on to work very hard in order to say a very little.

Many amusing incidents occurred among us, but I will relate but one.

In 1859 Mr. Levings was director of the school district, and I was clerk. One day in the early autumn, when I was particularly busy in my office, a young man named George W. Witherell came to me and wished to engage to teach the school during the coming winter. I did not like his appearance, and had no idea of hiring him, and so told him he had better see the director. He asked me to accompany him, but I excused myself on account of my urgent business. He persisted in his request, until I was fairly obliged to comply, and, in no very good humor, I started with him for Mr. Levings' house, about one-third of a mile distant. I had been showing him some of my best specimens of stammering, and, when near the house, I remarked that he might have observed that I had a hesitation in my speech. He said he had observed it. I told him I was afflicted that way, but Mr. Levings was a very rapid talker, and between us we averaged good time. We found him painting his house; he came down the ladder, and I introduced him, making fearful work of the job.

"Mr. Le-Le-Levings, l-let me ac-ac-ac — let me ac-acquaint you with Mr. W-Wi-With — with Mr. With-With-Witherell."

Levings looked at him, then looked at me, and began :

"Wh-wh-wh-*what* na-a-a-ame did you sa-a-a-ay?"

He wrestled fearfully with that first word "what." The contortions of his face were frightful to Witherell and amusing to me. Mr. Witherell did not get the school. I think he was resigned ; I don't think he wanted it very much after we had stopped talking to him ; but I had my revenge on him for taking me from my work.

For myself, within the year past, the habit of stammering has nearly forsaken me. I have taken no special pains to secure this result, and hardly know whether to rejoice at it or not. I shall try to retain enough of the habit to "sample" it when desired, though I should not indulge in its habitual use.

The years work their slow but certain changes, and man ripens for the grave as leaves and fruit do for their fall. The weakest leaves fall first, and it may be that this habit, the least essential of what is personal to myself, is thus the first to pass away — the first indication of that coming change, which, in God's own time, will bear us all over to that other life where no stammering tongues are found, but where language is music, life is thought, and law is love.

THE NEWSPAPER.

[Extracts from an address delivered before the Convention of the Minnesota Editors and Publishers' Association, held at St. Paul, June 4, 1870.]

There are some things from which the freshness never fades away — out of which the wonder never dies. Day by day we may stand beside a telegraph operator, but the mystery of his performance never becomes clear, and the sensation of surprise is always fresh and keen.

Just so the newspaper is a constantly recurring miracle whose wonder never wears away. Whether lying carefully folded in the office, or invitingly open upon the table; whether wrapping cheese and cod-fish, or thrown discarded into the street to scare horses and be trampled on, it is always invested with a strange kind of awe.

The newspaper! Look at it. It seems empty and vacant, perhaps. "Nothing in the paper," you say; yet read, and you will find it an open letter from very many people whom you have never known.

One offers you this commodity, and another that; one happy man sends you notice of his wedding, another sorrowfully informs you of a death. Look over its contents closely — its news items, its list of accidents, of fires, of crimes — see how sudden wealth has surprised some, and sudden poverty saddened others. Is it in war time? — look at the list of killed and wounded; see who has been promoted

and who disgraced; take into your mind the import
of the consequence of all these things, and you will
find that you hold in your hand "the ends of myriad
invisible, electric conductors along which tremble
the joys, sorrows, wrongs, triumphs, hopes and de-
spairs of as many men and women," all as sensitive
to pleasure or pain as yourself.

Here you have the lore of the scholar and the
wisdom of the sage. Here the divine preaches, the
poet sings, and the partisan lies. Here the states-
man proclaims his principles and the auctioneer
offers his wares. Here the Cardiff giant and Minnie
Warren are put side by side, and one is as long as
the other. Here is the result of the antiquarian's
research, and through the very next column throbs
a truthful tale of present love, passion and romance.
Here the Old and the New are brought into con-
trast. Here

> " Tradition, snowy-bearded, leans
> On Romance, ever young."

This is but a feeble portrayal of what a newspaper
is; let us now see how it is made.

Come with me to the office. We will pass that
pile of paper. Yet, stop; pick up a sheet of it. We
cannot wait to explain the curious process of its
manufacture, yet that clean and spotless sheet is the
purified product of rags and filth. The fibre which
forms its texture may have been stripped from Egyptian mummies; it may have come from city streets,
or from great garrets in country homes; it may have

wrapped the luxurious form of beauty, or been the scanty covering of want; but whether from the robes of a queen or the rags of a harlot, it gives no clue now to its former condition. Like a sanctified soul, it is ready for a new life.

We will pass the editorial room. Its occupants are busy. There are papers from far and near; letters from widely scattered correspondents; telegraph dispatches, intelligence in every form; and from this mass is to be selected what is of most interest and importance, to make a paper to-day. Let the editors work.

Come into the composing room. We have the foreman's permission — grudgingly given. Do you hear it? "*Click! click! click!*" What is that? Why, that is the music Progress marches to. Come here, to this "case." Look at that multitude of little boxes, filled with pieces of metal. What are they? They are the civilizers — they are THE TYPES. * *

But the paper is being made. The types, one by one, have been picked up by nimble fingers, and placed in proper position. Every error has been corrected. Every punctuation point is in its place. The scattered "columns" are massed together; the "form," or page, is securely "locked up," and sent to the press room.

Let us go there. Here is where the wondrous transformation is wrought; here matter becomes the exponent of mind. The "forms" are properly placed. The great press slowly moves; its arms are reaching for their strong embrace.

" Stop the press ! "

The giant rests again.   There is an error of statement to be corrected, or an objectionable article to
be withdrawn.   The types are taken out and borne
away — corpses of a dead thought.

Look now, again, at that mass of type—dead ! inert
as the earth you tread on.   But see, the white sheet
has fallen upon their upturned faces — the touch of
the Press has baptized them — the life that was in
them has passed upon paper, and the new creation
is pregnant with thought ; a thing with a soul, for it
can move the souls of men.   That sheet, so blank before, is a living power now.   A change has passed
over it, as marvelous as if, in an instant, the unwritten face of the boy should put on the furrows of age,
the lines of care, the impress of manhood's experience, thought and toil.

Thus the paper is born, and goes out into the
world.   No messenger can overtake it.   Its utterance
is unalterable now.   It may be explained, but not
erased.   The printed word can no more be recalled
than the departed spirit can be wooed back to the
cold body which it has left.

Here, now, we have it—the newspaper !   Wonderful product of brain and toil !   One would think it
should be dearly bought and highly prized ; and yet
it is the cheapest thing in the world.   Five cents will
buy it.   One or two dollars will bring it to your
home every week in the year.   And yet, strange to
say, there are men " too poor to take a newspaper !"
They can pay five cents for a glass of beer, or fifteen

cents for a beverage of unknown composition, called a "cocktail;" they can pay fifty cents for a circus ticket, or a dollar for the theatre, yet they are *too poor* to buy a newspaper! — a newspaper, which is a ticket of admission to that great Globe Theatre, whose dramas are written by God himself, "whose scene-shifter is Time, and whose curtains are rung down by Death!" * * * *

IF there is one lesson which life teaches more plainly than any other, it is the subordination of individual to general interest. Humanity is large; a single life, even the largest, is small. Engrossed with our daily duties, pressed by cares, and weighed down by exacting obligations, we often fancy that our life and labor is a very necessary and important thing. Yet a little reflection will show us that the world easily adjusts itself to its losses and life whirls on the rapid eddies and rushes in strong currents, and the express wagon jostling against the hearse, the black plumes threading the gay and busy crowd, who scarcely note their passage, or think that soon the same offices must be performed for them.

The sea smiles no less brightly in the sunlight because a dark and ghastly wreck lies hidden beneath its shining surface, and so the smile of life is scarcely saddened, or its hues robbed of their brightness, because of the awful shadow of death, which is its constant attendant. Humanity is large; individual life is small.

A BRILLIANT WEDDING. — Such is the caption of
the article before us; and then there is a description
of the attire and appearance of the bride, as minute
in regard to her "points," as an article in Wilkes'
Spirit, about the "points" of a favorite of the turf;
and a list of the bridesmaids is given, and how they
were dressed; and the trappings of the altar, and the
dignified grace of the clergyman, the brilliant music,
and the flowers, and the delighted and distinguished
guests, and the——; yes, there was a bridegroom; and
perhaps he loved his wife; and possibly, in spite of
all this glare and glitter, she loves him. We hope so.

We read of such weddings often — or rather, we
see the announcements and omit the reading. And
as we see them we wonder — wonder whether love
thrives best under the glare of such publicity —
wonder whether the splendor of the ceremony is
matched by the trustfulness of feeling and the purity
of heart which alone give to marriage vows their
sacredness, and assure a future of ever increasing
love and devotedness. We wonder whether the
country maiden, whose love grows as the violet does
— blushing at its own wealth, and shrinking timidly
from exposure,— whether she is not happier in the
quiet possession of her great treasure, than are the
darlings of fortune, whose loves are blazoned to the
world. Is the quiet contentment of simple life really
preferable to the splendor of fashion and the show of
wealth ? Is the rose that blossoms in natural beauty
sweeter than art's painted flowers ? We sometimes
think so.

AGRICULTURE.

[The following is a beautiful, quaint and humorous preface to a very practical address delivered at an Agricultural Fair.]

The Fair is the flowering time of the year. It is the Festival of Labor. Here industry exhibits its reward, Mechanism displays its triumphs, and Art receives her crown. All the long year the wondrous alchemy of nature has been patient at its subtle work, perfecting the results which we witness now. Winter snows have fertilized brown tilth and grassy sod; summer suns have led the springing stalk to its full stature, and hardened the milky berry into golden grain and ripened ear; Spring has flung out her blossoms with prodigal profusion, and Autumn, with pride, collects the ripened fruit, grown ruddy in Summer's fiery mould.

This is the season of fruition, and the Fair is a large and generous "Harvest Home," where each, in an honorable spirit of emulation, competes for supremacy in a field where the competition itself is of far greater value than the prize bestowed. Here is the romance of Labor. The best of the field, the first of the flock, the most skillful work of the hands, is exhibited here; and giving an added charm to all, is the social intercourse, so general, free and unrestricted upon every holiday of this kind. Other festivals are local or personal in their significance, and narrow in their scope; this is broad as the necessities of man, and appeals to universal human nature's daily needs.

It has been said, in praise of agriculture, that it was "the primal occupation of man." According to sacred authority, this is true; but according to the same authority, the primal man was not a signal success as an agriculturist. No man ever had a better start in the world than Mr. Adam. He inherited an estate of unexampled extent; it was furnished with a large variety and number of stock; his orchard was filled with fruit of rare excellence, which had not cost him a tithe of the trouble and care which our fruit growers experience in bringing their favorites to perfection; he had no line fences to keep up; no highway tax to work out; no shiftless neighbors to borrow his tools and neglect to return them; no politics to distract his attention; no corner grocery or club house, to engage his time and capture his cash : no speculators to contend against in the way of prices; and no Charles Reade to beguile him with the "Terrible Temptation" of an exciting and worthless romance,— and yet he was not happy. His farm was overrun with weeds and thistles, and he finally lost his homestead, and was turned out bankrupt, to preëmpt on the barrens — like a "poor white" on an exhausted "clearing," in the pine woods of the Carolinas.

Notwithstanding this inauspicious beginning, agriculture rallied from its first disgrace; the pages of history, sacred and profane, are aglow with its praise, and poetry has ever found it an inspiring theme.

Following the line of sacred story, we find that when Capt. Noah, at the close of a very memorable cruise, left the sea, and walked forth upon the purified earth, he "began to be an husbandman." He seems also to have had the taste of a horticulturist, for he "planted him a vineyard," and went into the manufacture of wine; and here we grieve to say, that like many other men who have since been in the same business, he partook too freely of his own production.

Close following after, come the days of the Patriarchs; and the history of the world gives us no pictures more stately and grand than those of these nomadic chiefs, whose wealth was in flocks and herds, and whose titles to power were their own kingly attributes; nor has language ever told a sweeter story than that of royal-born Rebekah filling her pitcher at the well, and hastening, with gracious hospitality, to press its coolness to the stranger's lips.

All the early history of the world is redolent with the flavor of the fields. But, passing over many characters which stand out bold and prominent, I can merely allude to Prince Joseph, an ingenious youth of the royal family of Israel. The pet child of a wealthy father, and the envy of less favored brethren, in his musings in the fields he formed a character whose robust virtue delivered him from the servitude of Pleasure, and in later life he developed a faculty for financiering which enabled him to assist his impoverished relatives, and gave him a lasting

fame.   He became one of the heaviest corn brokers
on record, and if not a veritable "bull" in the mar-
ket, he used a remarkable "corner" greatly to his
advantage, and like many men in later days, became
immensely wealthy by means of a government
contract.

Farther down the track of time, we find the touching tale of the Moabitish damsel, filial Ruth.   We
see her, with modest mien and downcast eye, glean-
ing the barley stalks; and mark her pleased surprise
at the kindness which finds and the love which follows her, and we love to remember that this poor,
dutiful, early widowed harvest girl, who shyly sat
beside the reapers, and shared their frugal fare, became the wife of princely Boaz, and the grandmother
of that great Hebrew bard and king whose songs
to-day make music in every sanctuary, and melody
in every Christian heart.

In a great, tumultuous assembly, when the *one man*
whom all are expecting approaches, all tumult ceases,
all sounds are hushed.   So in the still night watches,
when the hum of traffic and the din of toil has
ceased, and the weird and wondrous beauty of nature
sleeps in silence, seen only by the mild moon and the
sentinel stars, heaven stoops low to earth, and God
visits the world.   Then there is worship in the very
air.   The stones repeat their silent sermons — the
leafy boughs sway in unwritten melodies, and the
unvexed waters murmur musically to the shores.

A PREFATORY LETTER.

My Dear Joe:

This chip-basket is, or it should be, like an easy, gossiping letter to a friend. Do not you and every one else, often meet with pleasant passages which you wish to read to some one, and have quaint fancies flit across your thought, which you would like to imprison in words and write them to a friend? Well, this "Chip-Basket" is a collection of such fancies and such passages, and I, in thought, will send them to you, for your friendliness for myself will blunt the sharp edge of any criticism which another might indulge in. And if, occasionally, some thought should seem to demand a more elaborate statement than a "chip" could give room for, I can write it down here, and be as garrulous as I please.

And as I write now — the waning hours of the week drawing us close to the imaginary line which separates secular from sacred time — I think of another line, another boundary, which is not imaginary, but most solemnly real, towards which we are ever drawing near. It is the line which separates not only two countries, but two states of existence from each other, and from beyond which comes back to us no friendly greeting from those who have "gone before."

You know, Joe, that the traveler, in passing from one country to another, is often met at the boundary line by an officer, who strictly searches all his effects, to see that nothing contraband, or forbidden, is carried into the country to which he goes. How closely are guarded the boundaries of European kingdoms and empires; how the revenue officers guard the long line which separates the United States from the Dominion of Canada, to see that nothing is "smuggled" over; and in the late war, how searching the scrutiny and how constant the care that nothing "contraband" should pass to the hostile lines. The smuggler, the spy, and even the incautious traveler, are often loaded with treasures they would not carry if they knew they must be surrendered. Sometimes they pass undetected; sometimes the law enforces its penalty.

But that other boundary line to which I have alluded, is guarded with a vigilance that never ceases — with a vision that is never dim — an intelligence that never errs — a faithfulness that never fails. No mistakes are made; no wrongdoer passes undetected. That sleepless sentinel is the Angel of Death. No illusion cheats his eye. All deceit and subterfuge and hypocrisy stand revealed before him, and the man is simply the man himself. Virtue and honor, and love, and truth, and gentle charities, and Christian deeds, they are passed by the shadowy guard with an approving smile; but the ill-gotten gains of an unhallowed life are indignantly wrenched away, and their possessor held for impartial trial and inexorable doom.

TOOTH PULLING.

[The following was an impromptu speech made at a convention of the State Dental Association of Wisconsin, held in La Crosse in 1870:]

M-MR. P-PRESIDENT AND G-G-GENTLEMEN:

I have n-noticed in the p-papers that the "tooth pullers" of the State were to meet in council here at this t-time; b-but I had no desire for an introduction to their f-fraternity, and no e-expectation of being p-present at any of your s-sessions, until, t-through your urgent invitation, M-mr. President, and your reassuring terms, by which you quieted my nervous a-apprehension, I was induced to come in and hear the discussion of t-to-night. My l-love for your profession is not "greater than the love of w-woman," and if you, gentlemen, are of the same cloth as the d-dentist I first had an i-introduction to p-professionally, I should hope you would move a speedy and early adjournment, and depart from the city! I was more confiding when I met that d-dentist than I think I am now. He was one of those f-fellows who s-seem to h-have a "roving commission"—c-came to the place where I resided, and t-took a great deal of interest in me from the start. He was a brother m-mason, too, and secured my young affections. He w-wanted to look at my m-mouth, and, in a moment of w-weakness, I l-let him. Up to that t-time I thought my m-mouth was all

right — as good a one as I wanted.   But he found
only d-dire disaster there!   One tooth I must let
him pull, and at once, or ir-irretrievable ruin would
be the consequence.   I h-hesitated — and you know
what becomes of those who hesitate.   He seemed a
messenger sent just at that time to save my health
from impending r-ruin.   He was, of course, a superior d-dentist, for I had it *from his own lips*.

And then came out the strange instruments, more
d-diverse in appearance than what Peter saw let
down in a sheet — and all formed, it seemed, for the
especial purpose of saving my health from r-ruin.
He used those instruments.   I had a consciousness
at the time.   I th-think he e-explored the nerve,
and whatever else was in that tooth.   And then he
brought out g-gold, and then he punched it into
the tooth by the foot and by the yard, until I felt I
had a bank of deposit on which I could draw for
almost any "rainy day."

With bright visions I went to bed that night, but
not to sleep.   There was something worse than his
instruments gn-gnawing at that tooth.   I tried different combinations and m-modifications of these, but
I c-continued unhappy.   In the morning I sought
my dental friend, but he was not.   He had gone on
his mission to bless humanity in other p-parts.   It
were well thus.

I have no memorandum detailing exactly what I
did that day; I d-didn't forget that tooth!   In the
afternoon I anxiously sought the services of a sur-
geon who p-pulled teeth, and urgently requested him

to remove that tooth with or without the head. I
cannot describe his operation. I know h-he took
hold of it. I felt him. He p-pulled, and I p-pulled.
As a man of truth, I would say it didn't hurt, but
the astronomical observations I m-made at the time
were varied and extensive. When he got tired of
pulling, I put up my hand to let him rest. At the
third t-trial I remember there was a decided change
in the sensation; t-there was a deep-seated convul-
sive effort produced on my system which reminded
me of m-many I could not recall, and the tooth came
out! But I have st-stuttered ever since!

TO ——

Fair maid, although I dare not hope
   That thou of me art dreaming,
Although thine eyes may not with love
   On me be fondly beaming;
Though I may have no power to wake
   Thy heart with wild emotion,
Nor hear thy low voice breathe to me
   The vows of deep devotion;

Yet loyalty to highest art
   Sees beauty, where'er shining,
And, with a reverent eye and heart,
   Adores without repining;
And so, fair maid, I gaze on thee,
   And deem it no slight blessing
That I thy winning charms may see,
   Though ne'er dream of possessing.

HORACE GREELEY.

To say that Mr. Greeley had faults, is but to say that he was human. But whatever they were, his almost tragic death is the sublimest expiation which a noble soul could make, and has given convincing proof, if any were needed, of the purity of the motives which governed his life.

Mr. Greeley is equally great whether viewed as a journalist or as a man. He lifted journalism to a more beneficent position than it had ever occupied before. He made the " Tribune " not only a purveyor of news and advocate of a party, but a great educator and moral force. " His remarkable power, when traced back to its main source, will be found to have consisted chiefly in that vigorous earnestness of belief which held him to the strenuous advocacy of measures which he thought conducive to the public welfare, whether they were temporarily popular or not. Journalism may perhaps gain more success as a mercantile speculation by other methods; but it can be respected as a great moral and political force only in the hands of men who have the talents, foresight and moral earnestness which fit them to guide public opinion. It is in this sense that Mr. Greeley was our first journalist, and nobody can successfully dispute his rank, any more than Mr. Bennett's could be contested in the kind that seeks to float on the current instead of directing its course. The one did meet to render our American journals great vehicles of news, the other to make them controlling organs of opinion." ·

To this work he carried all the intense zeal of a propagandist. He was resistless in his advocacy of principles, although sometimes faulty in his methods of securing their fruits. He reached conscience, destroyed prejudice, and popularized conviction with equal success. "His rise from the printing-office to the editorial peerage, where he sat crowned and glorious in well-won laurels; his spotless private worth; his temperance, simplicity, and candor; his Franklin precepts for young and old; his love for his kindred and his friends; his war against slavery; his fight for exceptionless education and equality; his protest against legislative and municipal corruption; and his staunch championship of the rights of labor; — these are his titles of nobility, self-secured, brighter, and more enduring than if conferred by a college of kings."

Now, the man himself comes into view — the real Horace Greeley — "with his great active brain and tender heart, his grand hatred of wrong and charity for the wrong-doer, his tireless benevolence, and his unceasing labor for all that elevates humanity." His fame is immortal, for he linked his labor to immortal things. His life was given to crush the wrong, to defend the right, to educate the ignorant, to purify the vicious, to aid the weak, to uplift the lowly, to free the slave. The familiar " H. G." became a sign of almost cabalistic meaning, and it glowed on the pages of the " Tribune " an impulse and an inspiration to all noble struggling toilers for the right, as the cross shone on the banners of Constantine to cheer and strengthen the defenders of the church. Passing now into the August Presence, none will doubt that he has received the approving welcome, " Inasmuch as ye have done it unto one of the least of these my brethren, ye have done it unto me."

THAT man is truly thoughtful and humane whose sympathies are not confined to the circle of his own kindred, friends or acquaintance, but who, sitting securely in his own happy home, knows that wild hearts are throbbing in despair, sorrowful souls are suffering in silence, and pinched, wasting lives are weary in the struggle with want, in the great world outside his door. Through the full harmonies of his peaceful life there come ever to his ear the discords of sin and suffering in the great passion-tossed, tumultuous world. As a retired sea captain, spending the evening of life in some quiet inland home, hears, on stormy nights, the tumult of the sea, and feels a thrill of sympathy for the toiling ship and the brave men struggling to avert disaster and death; so the man who has felt the buffetings of fortune, or knows by observation how want and woe are the unvarying attendants of many who throng the paths of life, feels his heart go out in warm and active sympathy for all the poor and unfortunate among his fellow men.

THE TIN-PAIL BRIGADE.

A few mornings ago we were in Milwaukee, and at an early hour walked from the depot to the Newhall House. Early as it was, we had hardly ever before seen those familiar streets so thronged with pedestrians. We met the "tin-pail brigade" on their way to the entrenchments of labor.

These streets, which a few hours later would throb with the pulse of business activity, were nearly silent now, except where the hurrying laborers thronged the sidewalks, each carrying his ration for the day in the little tin pail. An hour later and these men would be invisible — hidden in shops and forges and manufactories, where all the long day they would toil, many of them for barely enough to supply themselves and those dependent upon them with the most absolute necessaries of life.

We thought we could read a great deal of the home life of each in the passing glance we gave as they went hurrying by. Here was one whose clothing was ragged and neglected, and on his face a hard, dissatisfied expression. It was easy to see there was no hope in his heart — that he went to his task as if it were a penalty imposed for crime, and that no pleasant and loving home life cheered him at the evening, and lifted from his heart the clouds that darkened his life. It is a terrible thing when the home of the poor lacks love, the only agency which can lighten its burdens and make it hopeful and happy.

Beside his walks another — no better, but much cleanlier clad, and the broad patches of his blue overalls are cleanly put on and not fringed with ragged edges. He has a home — you can see that — and, humble as it may be, there is a woman who is a confidant as well as a wife, and together they plan how to use their little means and increase their scanty store of comforts. They have ambition, and ambition to improve one's condition never fails to give force to character, and something of dignity and worth to life.

Here is a boy, too, not yet out of his teens, but there is something cheery about his countenance which shows that hope has issued him some drafts upon the future, and the thought of some good he is struggling for takes the bitterness from his life of toil. So the world goes — each heart lighted by some hope, as each home is lighted by a lamp of its own.

When we pass along the great business thoroughfares, and see the stately blocks rearing high their fronts adorned with elaborate and artistic workmanship, we do not think of the great strong blocks lying hidden in basement and foundation walls, upon which the weight of the whole superstructure securely rests. Just so does labor underlie the whole system of commercial and business life, and wherever are the homes of opulence and the palaces of trade, there, close by, are the scanty dwellings tenanted by the numerous families of the "tin-pail brigade." To narrow the distance between these extremes — to give capital the encouragement and protection to which it is entitled, and upon which its existence depends, and at the same time give to labor the best remuneration, the broadest field and the amplest opportunity possible, is the one great problem which the government has to solve to-day.

LINES

WRITTEN ON READING LINCOLN'S INAUGURAL ADDRESS.

On stormy seas our good ship sails,
 The breakers gleam along the shore;
She feels the breath of threat'ning gales,
 And quivers in the tempest's roar.

Now is our hour of utmost need
 We watch each strained and bending mast,
And saddened hearts in pity plead,
 " God save her till the peril's past."

But he who rules her deck to-day
 Is stout of heart and firm of hand,
And, mid the madd'ning tempest's play,
 Stands calm, courageous, fearless, grand.

Thank God! the hour has found the man,
 The night shall broaden into day;
Our land shall stand in Freedom's van,
 And Order reign, and Law have sway.

LIGHT. — What a wonderful thing is Light, which flows in upon us each morning as fresh as if new created, and steals away at night as slowly and regretfully as if that parting beam was its last! What a cheery philosopher is light! — always looking on the bright side of things, and bringing life and bloom wherever it goes. And what an artist it is! How it revels in the gorgeousness and delights in the delicacy of color! What a glory it throws on valley and hillside! How it stoops to deck the smallest flower with beauty, and searches out all penetrable nooks and corners and throws the smile of its gladness in upon them! How it lingers on the cheek of youth, tinging it with a bloom no painter can copy, and then — the daring artist — how it steals up to Beauty's lips, and leaves a crimson line on their very verge!

By the way, reader, did you ever reflect that a man or woman never gets over the childish fear of the dark? Reason and resolution may do much to control it, but fragments of our childish fears and superstitions cling to our stoutest manhood, just as at brightest noon shreds and patches of the night linger in shadow beneath the boughs of the thick-leaved trees. The darkness which hems in the day seems to be linked by mysterious influence to the darkness which circumscribes our lives, and vague fears, shadowy forebodings, ill-defined, unshapen fancies oppress us then, which we laugh at in the skeptical light of day.

REASON AND RELIGION.

We have no sympathy with that rigid, purblind righteousness which clothes itself in an impenetrable conservatism —which clings, with obstinate tenacity, to old beliefs —which believes every innovation on the established order of things to be of the devil, and so shuts its ears against all discussion. We are not to be frightened from the discussion of any important subject by the cry that the devil is one of the chief debaters. We remember that our blessed Saviour was accused as a blasphemer and Sabbath-breaker by the religionists of his day. We remember that all true progress in science and religion has been pointed out by those who were deemed foolish or mad, and that the great benefactors of mankind have been greeted with calumny and contempt. Speech, discussion is the wind that is to winnow the chaff from the wheat; and error cannot be confined in darkness, and rendered innocuous, but it must be vanquished in open combat, under the broad daylight of heaven.

For ourself, we have no craving desire to get a sight into the spiritual world. If there is any spirit who wishes to communicate to us anything important or beneficial, we should be most happy to pay him respectful attention; but we regard the practice and precepts of Christ as not only a safe, but *sufficient* law of life,— a law which, if obeyed, will bring blessing here, and added blessing hereafter.

We are not so ready to deify reason as some are. We have an idea that faith is not to be despised. Reason should be our guide in all matters which lie within its province ; but religion has mysteries which the human mind cannot fathom.   Reason and Religion never contradict each other; they run on in closest unity and most perfect harmony, until religion passes beyond the ken of reason, and there reason should merge into faith, even as the early light of morning melts into the splendors of broadening day.

WE speak of Columbus as the Great Discoverer, forgetful that all around us are discoverers greater than he.   He widened the horizon of the world for the people of his day, and for those who have succeeded them ; but the process of discovery has been continually going on, until now the clear eye of Science reaches to the centre of the earth, disclosing hidden treasures and mysteries, and successfully searches the far-off heavens, for stars and constellations unknown before.

Art has supplemented Nature with manifold wonders.   Invention has reinforced the strength and increased the power of man, until the world of Columbus' time is but an infant beside its manly stature of to-day.   Into this wider world every human being comes in perfect ignorance, and Life is but a Voyage of Discovery among its countless wonders.

Just watch the growing intellect of your child. The first blind gropings of mental activity are followed by that busy baby-life which is satisfied by

nursery toys.   Soon the increasing stature of the
little one is fitted for outdoor recreations, and acquaintance with the ever increasing circle of companionship begins.   What ardor and enthusiasm in
the youthful discoverer now!   How the larger
thoughts, the new ideas, throng to the recéptive
mind!   Every night shuts down upon a wider horizon; every morning beckons to new experiences and
untrodden paths.   Daily you can mark the mental
growth, and gladly note the joy of new discovery —
the enlarging life — the outreaching mind.

We are all but children of a larger growth, surrounded by outlying, undiscovered realms. Through
these we grope from day to day.   The farther our
vision reaches, the more we see beyond, just as the
sailor knows that, beyond the limit of the seeming
horizon that shuts him in, the waters are rolling in
wild waves, or sleeping idly in the sun.   Every day
increases our knowledge and ripens our experience.
Gulfs of unexpected faithlessness or hate yawn before us, and new loves and friendships join the procession of our lives.

Every night we are moored for a few hours by the
shores of Sleep, and with the break of every morn we
sail again upon the trackless sea of Time, piloting
our course as best we may towards the Wealth that
gleams in the distance — the Truth that shines se-
renely on the far horizon — the Beautiful, which
allures us with uplifted brow, persuasive smile and
beckoning hand.   Voyagers and discoverers are
we all.

12

GOD never forgets anything. All his works, from the creation of a world to the tinting of a leaf, are finished — perfect.

Did you ever stand under a full-boughed, heavy-foliaged tree in summer-time, and pluck one of its myriad leaves and examine its delicate tracery, its coloring, the very perfection of its finished beauty, and then think of the countless number of such leaves, of the mighty forests whose luxuriant growth covers so much of the world, and reflect that among them all there is not a leaf unfinished — each perfect in its form and color?

And did you ever pick a flower, either from cultured garden or by way-side walk, enjoy its odor and bless its beauty, and stop to think how all the wide earth blossoms with such fragrant beauty, and no flower of them all forgotten — the same careful hand filling each glowing heart with perfume and coloring every leaf with care?

When we think of this Omniscience, of this never-failing care, we feel something of the attributes of that Power — unseen, yet ever present; untouched, yet always felt — who gives to the violet its color, to the rose its fragrance, who tints with beauty the tiniest leaf, and yet whose hand controls the planets in their courses, and whose fiat rules the countless worlds.

IT is a fine thing to be able to ripen without shriveling; to reach the calmness of age, and still keep the warm heart and ready sympathy of youth.

BLIGHT AND BLOOM.

Never, in the history of the world, has there been a time when the terrible blight of life, home, happiness and possessions has descended upon vast numbers of people in such sudden and swift destruction as recently in our own Northwest, and never has there been a time when heroic fortitude and sweet and gracious charity have bloomed with a beauty so inspiring and glorious as now. Paradise was lost anew in the awful maelstrom of flame; Paradise was regained again in a vision of the millions of treasure spontaneously poured into the lap of suffering want, and the tens of thousands of feet all over the civilized world hastening with swift emulation in the work of mercy and fraternal human love. One picture is as if hell had burst its bounds, and ran in unchecked riot for a time; the next as if pitying heaven had touched every heart with the divine impulse to relieve the suffering and repair the loss.

It is impossible for words to portray either the darkness of the disaster or the brightness of the relief. The most eloquent description can no more picture the concentrated horror of the destruction of Chicago than a child's exclamation of wonder at a single star can portray the dazzling splendors of the countless suns and systems which fill the unexplored and unimagined boundaries of the universe of God. Looking back now at those blackened wastes and colossal ruins, they seem even more

mournful and impressive than when we wandered
through streets filled with the flying ashes of homes,
or clambered over the broken fragments of palaces
of trade, through which malignant flames still darted
their destroying tongues and hissed with scorching
breath.   Here the dread vision of the Apocalypse
was realized—the very rocks had melted with fer-
vent heat, and the treasures of art, the accumulations
of industry, the gains of commerce, were all rolled
together like a scroll, and heaped in one irremediable ruin.   There has been no scene of similar desolation since the ark rested on Ararat, and the dove
winged her weary way over a submerged world.

But if here was loss in gigantic form, and a horror
concentrated as never known before, in our own
State was a desolation spreading over a broader area
and marked by scenes more sickening and suffering
more intense.   Such a wave of hell as broke upon
doomed Peshtigo, and spread in fiery ruin over the
adjacent country, has not been known since God's
vengeance blotted Sodom and Gomorrah from
existence.   Who can conceive the surprise, the
struggle, the agony, the despair, the awfulness of the
situation and the powerlessness of the victims? Men
in their strength, women in their beauty, new-born
babes in their swaddling clothes, lovers in each
other's arms, corpses in their shrouds, and the coffined dead ready for the tomb, became flame and
ashes in the twinkling of an eye, while others baf-
fling the destroyer for a time, were at last caught in
his terrible grasp, and strangled in his embrace or

left writhing in an agony to which death would be welcome relief.

From such a picture it is sweet relief to turn to that sun-burst of sympathy which has illumined the world, and gilded our poor humanity with a glory unrecognized and unknown before. Then we found to what noble uses the telegraph and railroad might be put. Everywhere the lightning spoke the story of suffering and ruin, and brought back the response of sympathy and aid, and in every city and along every line of railway the great engines seemed to nerve themselves for a race to the aid of the houseless and hungry fugitives from flame. All ordinary feelings and interests were submerged in the one intense desire to render aid to those so suddenly stricken with overwhelming loss. No thought of church, creed or condition divided the force of feeling which filled every heart and found expression on every tongue. It was a new revelation of "good will to men"—a sublime translation of the gospel of Him who taught that it was more blessed to give than to receive, and who said that "Inasmuch as you have done it unto these, my brethren, you have done it unto me."

The response everywhere was so prompt, the relief so abundant, and the sympathy so sincere, that it seems useless to point out single instances, but one was so large that it well deserves mention.

At the first news of the calamity, the Erie Railroad made up a New York train, and sent its many agents and employés through the city gathering supplies. A few hours accomplished the work, and while this was doing, President Gould performed a work unequaled in the history of railroad management. All along the line his orders flew that the relief train had the *right of way*. And so it started, with relays of engines provided, and orders to make not less than forty miles an hour. Such a trip was never known before. The great freight trains sought the safety of side-tracks. The lightning expresses, with their mails and treasure, with passengers hurrying to meet business appointments, or intent on recreation — all stood still waiting for the passage of this unexpected train. Trade checked its impatience, pleasure forgot its disappointment, while mercy sped on, supplied with more than royal munificence and hastening with unimagined speed. It was a glorious thing to do.

So the one picture relieves the other. While the world is poorer to-day by millions of treasure and hundreds of lives, it is richer in the discovery of its own heroic qualities and saintly charities, and the conviction must come home with redoubled force to us all that, however poor and barren our individual lives may be, Humanity is heroic, affluent, large and warm.

DRESS is to a woman what binding is to a book — it may greatly improve the appearance, but cannot give increased value to the worth or worthlessness of that which it adorns.

RADICALISM.

The mass of timid and doubtful men, the men who were sure the Rebellion never could be subdued, the men who look on progress as necessary disaster, and to whom a hoary error is more sacred than a living truth, look on Radicalism as though it meant "chaos come again," and Radicals as though they were sacrilegious vandals wantonly plundering the Temple of Liberty. To their dim vision a Radical is a destroyer — whereas he is only the true renewer and builder.

You go through a street in a great city, and you see the workmen tearing down a building which has stood long and answered a useful purpose. What waste! What criminal destruction of property! you say. Not so. The old building is removed, the rubbish is cleared away, and a new, spacious and beautiful edifice is raised in its place.

Now, constitutions and laws are the house a nation lives in, the clothes it wears, and if there is growth in the people there must be change in the laws. Their spirit may not change, but their form must — just as the boy may wear the same kind of cloth after he becomes a man, but it must be cut by a larger pattern.

The Radical is not the vandal who sacks and destroys with no object but ruin; he is the wise builder who removes the old, which has been outgrown, and replaces in its stead the new, which is adapted to

present need.   In the fever and flush of a political
revolution, like that of the few years past, much that
is crude and unwise may be suggested by too enthusiastic leaders, but the people are pretty sure to act
with a wise moderation, in the spirit of true Radicalism.

. Radicalism is the synonym of all that is wise,
heroic and humane in the American politics of
to-day.

LOOKS UPWARD TO GOD.

[I turn then to the American people, and to that God who has never
forsaken them. — *Extract from Lincoln's speech at Columbus, Ohio.*]

There's a storm in the land threat'ning wide desolation,
   There's a must'ring of men, and a firing of blood ;
But trust fills our hearts, for the hope of the nation,
   The chief of our choosing, looks upward to God.

In the virtue of man and the blessings of heaven,
   His faith rests unshaken, his heart knows no fear,
For that God who the boon of our freedom has given,
   Will shine through our darkness, and smile on us here.

Then treason may mock — cursed sons of the nation
   May stab at the hand that has given them food ;
But the ark of our freedom stands firm and unshaken,
   For the chief of our choosing looks upward to God.

INFLUENCE OF LITERATURE UPON LIFE.

The fable of the "living tree, Igdrasil, with the melodious, prophetic wavings of its world-wide boughs, deep-rooted as Hela," has died out; but in its place we have the accomplished fact of the Printing Press, with wider influence than fable ever foreshadowed, with power more potent than Pagan philosophy ever dreamed of.

Much as is accorded to the press, men do not yet fully appreciate the controlling influence which Literature has upon Life.

Burke appreciated it when he said there were three estates in Parliament, but in the reporters' gallery there sat a *fourth estate* more important far than they all.

Mr. Southey understood it. "Literature will take care of itself," said Mr. Pitt, when applied to for some help for Burns. "Yes," added Mr. Southey, "it will take care of itself, *and of you*, *too*, if you do not look to it."

Carlyle saw its growing prospective power, when, thirty years ago, he proclaimed in his brave, resonant speech, "I say of all priesthoods, aristocracies, governing classes at present extant in the world, there is no class comparable for importance to that priesthood of the writers of books."

The art of writing—and of printing, which is a sequence to it,—is really the most wonderful thing in the world. Books are the soul of actions, the only audible, articulate voice of the accomplished facts of the past. The men of antiquity are dead; their fleets and armies have disappeared, their cities are ruins, their temples are dust — yet all these exist in magic preservation in the books they have bequeathed to us, and their names and their deeds are as familiar to us as the events of yesterday. And these papers and books — the mass of printed matter which we call Literature — are really the teacher, guide and law-giver of the world to-day.

You may judge a man more truly by the books and papers which he reads than by the company which he keeps — for his associates are often in a manner forced upon him, but his reading is the result of choice — and the man who chooses a certain class of books and papers unconsciously becomes more colored with their views, more rooted in their opinions, the mind becoming

> "Subdued to what it works in,
> Like the dyer's hand."

We have not space to specify the various proofs of the controlling influence of Literature. We can only state undeniable general truths. All the life and feeling of the young girl, fascinated by some glowing love romance, is colored and shaped by the page she reads. If it is false and weak and foolish, she will be false and weak and foolish too; but if it is true and tender and inspiring, then something of its truth and tenderness and inspiration will grow into her soul and become part of her very self. The boy who reads of deeds of manliness, of bravery and noble daring, feels the spirit of emulation grow within him, and the seed is planted which will bring forth fruit of heroic endeavor and exalted life.

TRUE FRIENDS.

MY DEAR JOE:

Did you ever think how transitory most of the friendships of life are — how very slight the tie that binds us even to those whose company we enjoy, and whose pleasure we would promote? How easily change of place or circumstance crowds out the old occupants of the heart and welcomes new ones in! We are surrounded with pleasant people, their society fills a large place in our lives, their respect and esteem is highly valued, we are glad to receive and render favors; but let us be removed from them but a short distance, just so that the orbits of our daily life do not intersect each other, and somehow they fade imperceptibly but surely away, just as the mist fades or the closing day darkens.

And the dead — they whose life, while living, seemed a necessity to our own, and whose death was like an eclipse of all our joyous being — how easily we become accustomed to their absence, and daily duties and new-found loves bridge over the awful chasm and fill the gloomy chaos which their departure made.

But some friendships live; some loves take such deep hold upon the heart that

> " Time but the impression stronger makes,
>   As streams their channels deeper wear."

Did you ever go into some rich old picture gallery, Joe, where the walls were hung with glowing master-pieces of nature and life — grandeur to awe the soul, and beauty to delight the eye, and where the ceilings were illuminated by the hand of genius and radiant with the very smile and triumph of art? Those pict-ures come and go. Where you find a favorite to-day a new-comer will hang to-morrow; but the frescoed miracles of art stay steadfast in their place. No change disturbs them, but there they remain, grow-ing ripe and mellow with age.

Just so it is with the heart. Many pleasant occu-pants come and go, but there are those who stay, like the frescoes on the walls and are an integral portion of the heart itself. He who has such friends — whose memory is a picture gallery, where in frescoed beauty smile the faces of unfading love — is rich indeed, rich in goods that cannot be purchased in the mar-ket, and whose value does not fluctuate with the price of gold. That you and I, Joe, may have such friends, and deserve them, is the wish of   LUTE.

A DOCTOR is continually standing upon the con-fines of existence — welcoming the new-comer, bid-ding farewell to the goer-away.

ART.

There is a great deal of humbug about what is called Art. It is regarded as "nice," and for its sake the fashionable lady endures an opera which she cannot comprehend, and the school miss works impossible animals in stunning colors. Men will crowd a theatre to see the representation of Medea — a roused, passionate woman — and applaud the mimic representation with delight, when very likely many of them, if at home, could witness the reality itself without the expense of buying a ticket. Look at pictures. A short time ago we were all enthusiastic over Prang's chromos of ducks and chickens. How foolish to purchase the picture, when we could buy the live chicken for less money, which would be at least fully as "natural" as the picture, and, after having admired its beauty, we could broil its body and gratify the taste with its delicate flavor, thus making it serve a useful as well as æsthetic purpose! — like the South Sea Islander, who patiently listens while the missionary strives to enlighten his benighted mind, and then coolly carves and cooks the preacher and appeases his hunger with the savory joints. Just now Correggio's " Magdalen " is a great favorite. The picture is rich, voluptuous, fascinating. But we suppose there are very many fully as beautiful and finely formed young women alive to-day — yet their friends would hardly advise them to adopt the scanty costume and *abandon* of manner which is ad-

mired in Magdalen, who probably was not a very
nice, fastidious girl.   Look at landscape paintings.
People will go into ecstacies over an impossible landscape hanging on a parlor wall, who are blind to the
wondrous exhibitions of nature around them, and
never lift their sleepy eyes to that wondrous picture
gallery, the sky, which God's mighty hand fills day
and night with forms and colors of ever-changing
glory and gloom.   Art is valuable only as an incentive to observe, and a help to appreciate nature.   It
should be a means, not an end — the priestess in the
temple service, not the goddess to whom adoration
is given.

TO DESDEMONA.

Thou bright creation of the poet's mind!
In thee did his great soul express
Its fairest type of female loveliness.
In thee all feelings pure, refined,
Do dwell.   Each inmost thought of thine
Is holy as a saint's rapt dream of heaven,
While every outward charm to thee is given.
As timid buds blush coyly into bloom,
So do thy modest virtues show their worth;
And as the full flower sheds a rich perfume,
So doth thy presence beautify the earth.
Oh, winning Teacher! Thou didst well fulfill
Life's holy mission, and though dark thy fate,
Yet from thy pure life will we still
Learn to love virtue *for its own dear sake.*

THE TRIUMPH OF PRINCIPLE.

[Written upon the occasion of the dissolution of the American Anti-Slavery Society.]

The world has seldom witnessed a more imposing sight than the grand military review at Washington at the close of the late war. The victorious veterans of the army of the Republic, bronzed by sun and battered by fight, swept in triumphal procession past the pleased eyes of chiefs and civilians, and brave men paid them heartfelt homage, and lovely women gilded the glory of their achievements with the brightness of beauty's smiles. The sight was grand and inspiring, and when that mighty army so suddenly melted away — the resistless soldiers becoming quiet, peaceful citizens once more — the world looked on in wonder, and marveled at the flexibility of our national life, and at the almost miraculous completeness of the change.

But there was another "muster out," a few days since, no less full of significance. It lacked the pomp and circumstance of the Washington review — its soldiers wore no uniform, but they were veterans none the less. It was the dissolution of the American Anti-Slavery Society. That society has been engaged in a forty years' war, and there were veterans at the final muster out who had been among the earliest enlistments.

In its infancy, the members of that society en-

dured contumely and hate, they were the objects of
reproach and scorn, they suffered personal indignity
and were exposed to personal danger.   Unseduced
by the blandishments of social position, and unal-
lured by the temptations of political power, they
followed where duty led, as grandly as Israel followed the cloudy pillar and the flaming guide — for
they knew that, as of old, God was in the van, and
his people would not suffer loss.

By-and-by conviction came to the multitude, truth
was triumphant, and tardy honor kissed the veterans'
brows.   They lay off their armor now, for the victory
is complete, the work is done.

THE BANNER.

[Written on the occasion of the presentation of a prize banner by the
State to Pierce county, Wis., for the best display of farm products at the
State fair.]

Thou wast not won on bloody field,
　　Where murderous hosts in conflict meet ;
But where the long broad furrows yield
　　Their yellow wealth of ripened wheat.

Now Honor sits on Labor's brow,
　　The golden days return again ;
And Science fair shall guide the plow
　　Which turns the brown tilth of the plain.

Peace hath her victories, and the land
　　Which honors thus her sons of toil
Shall never want a willing hand
　　To guard or till her fruitful soil.

THE WANING YEAR.

" The year growing ancient,
  Not yet on Summer's death, nor on the birth
Of trembling Winter."
                        —*Shaks. Winter's Tale.*

Autumn is the season of fruition, recompense, reward. Spring is the time of promise; Summer, of busy fulfillment; Autumn, of ripened, perfected fullness and possession. In Autumn nature pays the bills which have been drawn upon her through the year, and decks herself with lavish expenditure and more than royal pomp and beauty.

June is full of fragrance and subtle beauty, but October is ripe, sensuous, glowing, imperial. On these warm, hazy days, when the sunlight kisses but does not scorch, when the very streams seem to meditate as they murmer along, when wood-crowned bluff and hillside glow with every imaginable color, and the soft haze, like the veil of a bride, heightens the beauty which it half conceals,— on such days the lost Eden seems restored again, the old poetic traditions of mythology revive, and wood and field and spring and glen are sanctified by the presence of attendant deities who whisper their secrets into willing ears. It is a "liberal education" to be abroad at such a time, providing only one has the eye to see the unexcelled and ever-shifting panorama of beauty, and the heart to treasure up its wonderful revelations.

13

One fact cannot fail to interest the observer, and that is the uniformity of the "fall fashions" for bird or beast or field or tree. The prairie chicken, which peers at you from the tall grass, is the same color as it; the partridge, which scurries away through the thick underbrush, is scarcely distinguishable from the foliage which covers its flight; and even the chipmunk, which chippers at the base of the great bluff, wears in his own striped coat the colors of the oak, the maple and the sumach which glow so gorgeously above him.

One views, too, with an admiration which deepens into awe, the perfection everywhere manifest. No mistakes or incompleteness here. That great Power for whom innumerable temples are built, to whom perpetual prayer and praise ascends, and who holds uncounted worlds in his keeping, does not neglect the fashioning of the most slender stem, or the tinting of the tiniest leaf.

A SHORT time ago we were one of a small party which visited a beautiful cemetery lying in the lap of majestic mounds, and looking out upon a fair city and a broad reach of prairie and river. Nature had made this a lovely spot, and art had added to its attractions. The sunlight lay warm upon shapely evergreens and carefully tended flowers, and the spot looked indeed like a place of rest, where, "after life's fitful fever," one might sleep sweetly and well.

Winding around and up the stately bluffs were carriage ways of easy grade, and, terrace above terrace, bank above bank, rose the pillared massive monuments, or gleamed the humbler marble slabs. But more affecting than the most costly memorial which wealth had placed over the last resting place of its loved, were the frequent little mounds, newly made, which told where a mother had laid her child down in the embrace of that kindly Earth which is mother of us all. And then we thought that these sun-warmed, flower-fringed banks of earth were banks indeed, banks where we deposit our choicest treasures, and in whose silent vaults they shall safely lie until the resurrection morn. And the mothers who silently bore their darlings here — we could not think of them as impoverished and bereft, but rather as the royal possessors of blessed memories and of treasures deposited, safe from all possible disaster or loss, which should be returned to them in heaven. The balance of the bank-book is not so sure an index of garnered wealth as are the little mounds which break the graveyard sod into billows of green. O, better the mound and the marble than the living death which blights but does not kill. Better the sexton and the bell, than the slow decay of honor, the loss of love, the sunset of hope, and the darkening eclipse of life. The cemetery is not a synonym for sadness, nor the grave so dreadful as a stranded, rotting soul. Not all that marble covers was laid down in faith and love and tears, but we know the *little* mounds cover only what was precious, pure and fair.

THE BLACK CROOK. — Its plot is moral. Fiends and fairies struggle for the possession of a noble human soul, and the fiends get badly euchred. This is excellent, and gives a man's good resolutions a healthy jog.

Its pictures, sometimes called scenery, are very gorgeous and glowing, and have an excellent moral. Hell is a fearful ugly place, and the abodes of the fairies, or spirits of good, shine with splendor, like a row of tin pans in the summer sun. The wicked old Black Crook is toasted like a muffin on Zamiel's trident, and the virtuous Rodolph has a good time of it with Stalacta and the rest of the girls. In brief, the pictures forcibly portray the sinfulness of sin, and the blessedness of being good.

Its ballet has been supposed to be somewhat demoralizing. It is not. It is as proper as a girl's recess at a district school in the summer time. The dresses of the dam—sels are uselessly long, for the lower limbs shown on the stage are no more seductive than the legs of Rus. Munger's pianos, or the legs turned out by a lathe machine. This can be relied on.

The Black Crook may be slightly seductive as performed in New York, but I am proud to call attention to the superior morality of the West, and the tribute which Mammon pays to the virtues of St. Paul, in that in deference to the pure and healthy tastes of her people, this play, as presented to them, is shorn of all appearance of evil, and is exalted into a great moral and almost evangelical agency.

CHRISTMAS AND CHRISTMAS GIVING.

What! Write about Christmas; that is an old subject to say anything fresh or interesting about. Yes, it is an old subject — not old as the world, but only old as He whose divine nature and transcendent work makes him hailed as the Saviour of the world. There are things older than Christmas which yet have the grace of youth and the freshness of a first experience in them. The morning, which breaks in light and wakes a world with impalpable touch, is older than Christmas, yet its beauty is fresh as when its beams first lit the abysses of chaos, and struggled through the misty shrouds of ancient night. The summer showers, which ride on sunbeams to the happy earth and steal in vapor back to the parent skies, are now as fresh as when flower or grass first brightened at their touch. That wondrous and inimitable artist, Frost, who covers in a few hours whole landscapes with a tracery more delicate, a finish more perfect than tiny brush of painter dare to emulate, he is older than the hills he crowns with snows, or the brooks whose babbling voice he stills.

No, Christmas really is not so very old, after all. It is an after-thought of time — one of the improvements of these later progressive days. Love, now and forever to be symbolized by a child, was old before the Star of Bethlehem blessed the earth with its rejoicing rays. The mother looked into the sweet face

of her babe, the youth walked with beating heart
beside the blushing maid, filial love tended reverently upon decrepit age — long before Mary sang her
low lullaby to the infant Jesus, or the wise men followed the star which led to where he lay.   Moses,
rocked by the reedy Nile, and watched by faithful
love; Ruth, following the reapers with modest mien
and downcast eyes; Esther, clad with the purple of
power, yet linked with unabating love to the lowly
people of her race — shall we forget or cease to listen
with rapt admiration to the simple annals of their
lives ? — and yet they all antedate Christmas by long
centuries of years.

No, the story of Christmas is new and ever will
be, for it is in the very essence of all things noble
and loving and pure that they laugh at time and
wear the coronal of youth forever.   And what so
noble as the life whose beginning Christmas commemorates ? — what so loving as that spirit which
has mellowed the asperities of life, and made one
birthday a universal festival ? — what so pure as the
doctrines of the Great Teacher who gathered into one
grand sheaf all the worthy maxims of morality and
rules of religion which had been taught by saint or
sage before him, and glorified them with a new splendor, and infused into them a breadth, a power, hitherto unapproachable and unknown ?

It is fitting that Christmas should be a day of
gifts — a holiday indeed.   It should be the world's
vacation from care, its festival of hope and joy.   We
are taught that divine beneficence found its highest

expression in the gift to the world of Him whom this day commemorates; so let the Christmas trees blossom with beauty, let the Christmas carols break into melody, and let happy childhood run riot in a joy whose meaning and explanation shall come to them in riper years.

LOAFERISM IS DEATH.

· "What is a man,
If his chief good and market of his time
Be but to sleep and feed?   A beast, no more."
—*Hamlet.*

Start not, reader, it is true.   Loaferism *is* death —death of the most dismal and dangerous kind. There are more kinds of death than one.   There is the death of the body, when sad farewells are spoken, when eyelids droop over sightless eyes, and pale lips close over voiceless mouths, when in silence and mid sorrow the stern agony is endured, and the light and warmth of life is exchanged for "the shroud, the pall, the breathless darkness, and the narrow house." This death alone is inevitable.   But as sunlight often gilds the mountain's top, around whose lower sides dark clouds are drifting, so is there a land of light and blessedness lying somewhere in the "Great Unknown."   But there is a death or torpor of the mind, a death of kindly affection, a death of generous trust and ennobling faith, a death of fixed purpose and noble endeavor which lead to a brightness beyond. Here is a business man, alive to the musical chimes of silver and gold, keen to detect the means of pecuniary gain. In his eager, untiring labor for wealth, he has forgotten the wealth of affection, the world of intellectual enjoyment which lies around him. The heart is dead, but a portion of his intellect is sharpened into unnatural life. Here is the ignorant day-laborer. He knows nothing of the wealth of science, the lore of history, or the charms of poetry. His mind is all uncultured and inert. But he is not wholly dead. His heart is alive. He loves his wife and joys in the sweet presence of his children, and labors cheerfully for their support. Here is another whose course in life is fitful and changing as April skies. He has no fixed purpose. He goes on like a sail-vessel driven here and there by every wind, and often becalmed — instead of moving steadily onward like a steamer breasting every opposing wave, and dashing aside obstacles as the steamer at every pulse-beat of its fiery heart dashes aside the spray. Some part of his manhood is dead. He has no faith in the omnipotence of work, no just conception of his dignity as man, no worthy goal in view, and so his course is vacillating and uncertain.

The loafer has suffered the triple death of heart, mind and purpose. He cannot love any one worthily, for love makes us self-distrustful, it awakens desire for nobler life, it inspires to work. He cannot even be a good friend, for his nature is too sluggish to perceive and meet the delicate requirements of friendship. His mind is dead, except that baser part which gives expression to passion and appetite. The dignity of man, the divinity of knowledge, the desirableness of self-culture, the unmeasured worth of the soul — all these inspiring thoughts are lost to him. O loafer! thou art a miserable being. Thy life is aimless as the beast's. Thou wilt gaze on life with an eye as dull as that of the ox who looks on a beautiful landscape.

Young man, would you be a loafer? It is a small task. "*Facilis descensus Averni est.*" "The way to hell (or loaferism, about the same thing,) is easy." You have only to hate to work, to neglect to cultivate your mind, to acquire a passion for playing all kinds of games and telling all kinds of stories, to allow yourself to hang around public places, and the thing is done. You are defunct, dead and worthless, and you bear about your own epitaph, written unmistakably plain — Loafer!

A FEW days ago, just as the sun was rising, in the stillness of the beautiful morning we heard the rumble and roar of a great train leaving the depot. Turning our eyes that way, we found the train itself concealed from view, but its progress was marked by the great bursts of smoke which constantly rose from the engine, marking the changing position and progress of the train. Never before have we seen such a trailing banner, full a mile in length, as that engine bore through the clear thin air of that wintry morn. Rolling out in great black billows, it would widen and whiten, unroll and spread, and pile up in fantastic shapes, only to unroll again and take on other shapes more fantastic still, still rising higher and growing more impalpable and clear, until at last it melted imperceptibly away, swallowed up by the surrounding air.

Looking at this wonderful, ever-shifting and ever-whitening panorama, we thought how like it was to the memory which a good man leaves behind him. Seen in the present, his life, at best, is full of imperfections, veined with black lines of selfishness, ambition or greed — but, as the years pass away, these fade out in the mellow light of time; we think and speak of them no more, and so at last his memory comes to be purified of all stain, and is ever after an inspiration for goodness and truth to all who think upon it; and the man himself, according to his position and influence, is enshrined in the love of friends and relatives, or taken into the world's wide heart, is canonized as a saint and made a potent power forevermore.   Happy they, be they humble or famous, who leave such memories behind!

FANCY is merely Fact coquetting a little with Falsehood.

TRAIN AND CHRISTIANITY.

[From an editorial reviewing a lecture by George Francis Train, so far as it alluded to the Christian religion.]

The Christian religion, as the abiding faith and the last enduring hope of all civilized mankind, is in no danger from Mr. Train.   What the deep and reverent skepticism of Spinoza, the monumental learning of Hobbes, the wit of Voltaire, the bitterness and malignity of Paine and the logic of Taylor have vainly assailed, will receive no detriment from the assaults of a man whose highest claims to public attention are found in the fact that his impudence and egotism render his ignorance amusing.

We do not mean to deny to Mr. Train the possession of an incisive wit, a vivacious and brilliant intelligence, and what has been aptly called "vast and varied misinformation," but his attempts to explain the origin of Confucius, Buddha, Zoroaster and Mahomet disclosed such utter ignorance of the subject as to create amazement even in the minds of his warmest admirers.

As already intimated, there was nothing original in Mr. Train's onslaught upon Christianity.   It was a sickly revival of old stock quotations and Joe Millerisms on the subject, which civilization has lived down—which the intelligence of the age, in harmony with its spiritual needs and resentments, has long since banished among the obscenities.

But while there is no danger to the body of Christian theology and the Christian institutions of the land, from such puny efforts as these, there is danger that thoughtless persons, like some who applauded the other evening, beguiled into hero-worship by the wit and " smartness " of the speaker, may have their faith unsettled. For a man who has been reared in the shadow of the church, who has found in its teachings alone the answer to his questionings of the hereafter — for such a man to be brought to ask that awful question, " Art thou he that should come, or look we for another ?"— and to go away doubting and unsatisfied, is the mournfullest thing that can befall a soul upon earth.

A religion — a belief in the fixed relations of all men to a universal divine government, and in a future state where imperishable souls will fulfill a destiny determined by their conduct in this — is as much a natural constituent of the human mind as will, memory or understanding, and the want of such belief as monstrous and abnormal as a condition of idiocy. Nothing proves this more clearly than the avidity with which men in all ages have embraced the impostures brought to them in the name of religion. Many of these impostures, like Mahometanism, have sustained polities and systems of government and forms of partial civilization for centuries. But in every case where they have not been discarded by the intelligence of the peoples holding them they have been discredited by the manifest superiority of other systems rising above them.

Eighteen centuries ago many such systems had perished, and their traditions were scattered through the silly fables of barbarism. The Greeks, and the Romans after them, had reasoned Jupiter out of existence, and while some of their wise men were attempting to make to themselves a new God out of philosophy, the masses were flocking in obedience to the uncontrollable instinct, around the impure altars of Phœnician and Egyptian divinities. Vice and ignorance on the one hand, and mere intellectual license on the other, rooted out the pristine virtues and the old faith of the people, and were preparing the way for the downfall of the ancient civilization. It was the age when skepticism stood ready to join hands with depravity.

It is not too much to say that the Christian religion which came in this Providential period, and in spite of fire and sword and persecution, in spite of the poverty, obscurity and weakness of its originators and adherents, fastened itself upon the times, intercepted the calamity, and preserved the world from barbarism. And from that period down to the present, it has been the founder of laws, the nurse of the arts, the forerunner and pioneer of the only form of civilization which promises the redemption of all men to higher and nobler life. And not only has it proved itself the great organizer of society and government, but in its influence upon individuals, in mitigating and soothing the asperities of existence, and lifting spiritual aspirations into definite assurance, it has shown itself the indispensable support of that humanity which is more important than government •and more enduring than society. Every good thing which is known to modern man, every social ordinance and public institution to whose care, as to an ark of safety, he commits his children, his country and his hopes, is involved, for good or evil, with the fate of the Christian system; and every thrust and stab at the integrity of that system is a blow at civil order and social safety.

What shall we have in its place when it is stricken down? Where is the philosophy, the code of merely human ethics without divine sanction, with power to dominate and unify the intellect of all men in its support, and restrain their lusts within those limits where alone civilization is possible? Is it in the twaddle of George Francis Train?—the airy refinements of Emerson?—the mysticism of Hegel and Fichte? But *every* man who has succeeded in stifling the cry of his heart for supernatural aid may assume his equality with the greatest of these, and reject the authority of each in his turn, and establish a code of ethics for himself. The intellectual perversities and delusions which must inevitably follow from such confusion of ideas and systems would very quickly demonstrate their own absurdity and perish, but in their fall might drag down to destruction the whole fabric of civil society.

Are those who applauded Mr. Train's speech the other evening prepared for the change? We think not. Let them be satisfied (as who is not?) of the deficiencies and imperfections of the church, and the misdeeds of many professing Christians — yet they will see, upon examination, that faulty as it is, its faults are in its administration and not in its origin or principles; that, faulty as it is, there is on earth for the soul of man no other refuge and no other hope.

We have penned these words, not as professing Christians, nor as men worthy either in character or conduct to stand for so great a cause, but from the standpoint of men of the world who would not willingly see destroyed the only existing guarantee of progress and civilization, and who, if they have not the grace to choose the better part themselves, yet cannot endure that all sacred things should be scoffed at in public places in a Christian land, by a man who boasts of his ignorance in those branches of learning most needed in order to judge of them, and whose most conspicuous trait is inability to comprehend that which he sneers at.

"ALL RIGHT."

There are some little phrases which occupy the same place in the coinage of words that dimes and sixpences do in the coinage of money. They are freely passed back and forth in the interchange of thought, and every one shares in their possession. Among these is the phrase "All right." Young America meets his fellow in the street, and accosts him with the customary "How d'ye do?" "All right," is the ready response. The merchant, counting the change for an article just sold, blandly assures the purchaser that it is "all right." You ask the steamboat clerk about your state-room, or the porter about your baggage, and receive the consoling assurance — "All right." A friend shows you a note bearing your signature, which he has just purchased. You glance at it, and, with the most perfect *sang-froid*, remark "All right." The train is filled with anxious and impatient passengers, the engine hisses and groans like a demon in pain, and its fiery heart seems to throb with anger at the delay, yet it stands motionless, waiting for the conductor's signal that "all's right." A short time ago we were driving along, and as we were going down a hill at rather a reckless speed, a sudden turn brought us into close proximity to another carriage loaded with ladies and gentlemen. A light shadow of fear and apprehension clouded the fair faces of the ladies, but as we whirled past, the hubs of the car-

riages merely giving each other a friendly rub, a
jolly, rollicking, good-natured looking fellow, whose
Young America hat sat jauntily on his head, pleasantly informed us that everything was "all right."
We had scarcely anything in our head but the end
of a cigar, and its mild influence induced a musing
mood — and so we fell to thinking whether our jolly
fellow had told the truth when he said "all right."
Did he realize the breadth and comprehensiveness
of that phrase? Was it "all right" with him? Were
his thoughts and actions toward that sweet-faced
girl by his side "all right?" Was his conduct toward
her that of manly honesty and noble reverence?
Were his thoughts chastened and ennobled by gazing
on her beauty, or was he toying with her to pass an
idle hour, watching with pleasure his power to call
the color to her cheek, and criminally waking up
emotions and feelings which must flow forth unmet?
In his relations toward the world was he "all right?"
Did he harbor no feelings of anger or resentment
toward any one? Was the "golden rule" the law
of his life, or was he selfish in his aims and purposes,
pushing his way to his desired goal, regardless of the
rights, the interests or the feelings of others? In his
relations to himself was he "all right?" Was he vio-
lating no law of his physical being? Was he always
true to his better judgment and noblest impulse?
Had the possibility of human culture, of a manly
and noble growth of soul, occurred to him? Was
his mind enriched and strengthened by calm reflection, by careful observation, by communion with the

14

great souls of the present and of past ages? Was his eye trained to see the beauty that greets us with all its freshness on each succeeding day? Did he rightly appreciate and enjoy

> " The glory of the sunset skies,
>   The tenderer beauty of the dawn?"

In his relations to the Great Maker of all was he " all right?" Was his whole soul permeated with a deep feeling of reverence and adoration as he looked up to the Giver of all good? Had he learned to "look through Nature up to Nature's God?" Did he

> " Love all virtue, like the light,
>   Dear to the soul as sunshine to the eye?"

In fact, was he, as he jocularly assured us, " all right?" And, thinking of him, we naturally inquired if with ourself it was " all right."

GRAVES AND GRAVEYARDS.

There is no way in which a refined and cultivated taste more appropriately shows itself than in adorning and beautifying the dwellings of the dead. The ancient Egyptians gave but little care to their earthly houses, but they spent years of toil and employed the highest artistic skill upon their tombs. There is a philosophy in this. We love to think of the dead as crowned with immortal beauty, as wearing the bloom and possessing the vigor of eternal youth. We forget the foibles and faults which might have been theirs, but the remembrance of their virtues and kindnesses dwells ever with us. And the spot where they are laid should be beautiful to the eye, be adorned by the hand of affection, that all our thoughts of the dead may be elevating, pure and pleasant. Then, too, a graveyard, if tastily kept, is always a place of resort, not only for those who have heart-treasures buried in its bosom, but for the stranger who may be "within our gates." Is it not fitting, then, that the graveyard should be made attractive, that its location should be pleasant, that it should be adorned by art, that flowers and beautiful shrubbery should spring from the soil where lie the "dear departed"—so that to one gazing upon the scene, death should be robbed of some of its asperities, and, as he thinks of the time when his cheek shall be colorless and his eyes closed forever, he will

be enabled to look with quiet resignation, with subdued and chastened pleasure,

> " Into the great Unknown,
> Into the silent land?"

Notwithstanding the sneers of the skeptic, the
heartless philosophy of the stoic, and the faith of
the Christian, death is an event almost universally
dreaded. It is not the agony of dissolving nature
which we fear, but it is the sense of that mystery
which shrouds our exit from this world and entrance
upon another. Even he who trustingly confides in
the Scriptural revelations of a future world, is awed
and startled by the very grandeur of those revelations, and he passes into the portal of death with that
trembling hesitation with which a peasant would
enter the palace of a king.

But it is in our power to rob death of many of its
unnatural terrors. The graveyard should be made
so attractive as to become a pleasant place of resort,
and so gradually the idea of death will become do-
mesticated in our minds, the "better land" will
become more familiar to our thought, and the conviction will live more constantly within us that we
"are passing through nature to eternity." We have
passed many pleasant hours in graveyards. As we
now write there are touching and beautiful scenes —
and some sad and sorrowful ones — which memory
brings vividly to mind. But it would protract our
article too far to relate them.

Yet we cannot close without enriching our page

with a passage from Shakspeare, a passage which has elicited the admiration and touched the feelings of thousands, a passage which will command the praise and call forth the sympathy of men and women as long as genius shall be prized, and the heart be moved by the tear of sorrow and the sob of grief— the burial of Ophelia.

Ophelia needs no eulogy. To know that Hamlet loved her is a sufficient guaranty that she possessed all sweet and maidenly qualities. Yet, thinking of her burial, we love to think of her life, of her filial obedience, of her maidenly love, of her sweet praise of the loved one, of her touching lament over his supposed madness, of the last sad scene when, "chanting snatches of old tunes," she sank to "muddy death." We think of Hamlet too—of the thoughts and emotions which must have crowded upon him as he talked with the grave-diggers, soliloquized over the skull of "poor Yorick," and watched that form laid in the grave in which had been garnered up all his youthful loves.

The reluctant priest has performed the obsequies. She has had

> " The maiden strewment, and the bringing home
> Of bell and burial."

When Laertes asks :

> " Must then no more be done?
>   *Priest.* No more be done :
> We should profane the service of the dead

To sing a requiem, and such rest to her
As to peace-parted souls.
   Laer. Lay her i' the earth;
And from her fair and unpolluted flesh
May violets spring! I tell thee, churlish priest,
A minist'ring angel shall my sister be
When thou liest howling.
   Ham. What, the fair Ophelia!
   Queen. (*Scattering flowers.*)
Sweets to the sweet: Farewell!
I hoped thou shouldst have been my Hamlet's wife;
I thought thy bride-bed to have decked, sweet maid,
And not have strewed thy grave."

THE HOLIDAYS.

The week intervening between Christmas and New Year's is the week of gladness, joy and fruitage. The blessings which the year has borne, the good it has wrought, finds expression in Christmas gifts and New Year's presents, and the love which proffers these, and the thankfulness which accepts them, is more to be valued than the gifts themselves.

Love is to the life of the soul what electricity is to the world of matter — an unseen, all-pervading and almost almighty force. With it life blossoms into beauty, and is fragrant with mystic meanings and rich in noble uses. Without it life is dead as a sapless trunk, cold as a corpse.

But love cannot always run on its sweet errands. Daily duties, stern necessities, the imperative demands of life, often confront it. Limited means make it impossible to translate the generous thought into equally munificent action. And so, as the year stores her warmth and light, her flavor and lustrous beauty into the ripening fruit and drops it in autumn, mellow, sweet and golden, into waiting hands, so love garners its gifts until the Christmas ushers in the week of joy and thankfulness, and then proudly places them in expectant hands, and reads its reward in the light of eyes sparkling with pleasure, or dimmed with a happiness which forces tears. The holidays are the harvest-time of human love.

Now, too, we "post the books"—not the ledgers alone, but the account current of our lives—and see whether we are drifting toward yawning gulfs of sin, or rising with purer purpose toward nobler life. Of course one day is like another, and our division of time merely an arbitrary one, but yet in the future, as in the past, the advent of the New Year will continue to symbolize the youth of the world, the perennial joy of creation, the immortal spirit that, amid the ravages of death and decay and care and sorrow, still pursues its course to its celestial destiny.

AN EDITOR AND HIS PAPER. — A newspaper is not a person, but it is considerably more than a thing. It has a separate existence, an identity distinct from that of its editor or publisher, though its life is very closely connected with the brain of the one and the pocket of the other. It may be an object of love and respect, or of hatred and detestation. The relation between an editor and his paper is something which neither Webster nor Worcester has fully defined. The paper is not the editor, though it demands his care and absorbs his thought, hanging on to him like a poor relation, as dependent as a participle on its parent verb. It interprets his ideas, and reflects his life — is a sort of errand boy, carrying his thoughts, — and has, moreover, a wise reticence, never communicating anything concerning its editor except what he wills to have known. The editor may be a harum-scarum fellow, with many little flaws on the surface of his daily life, but the paper is sober, staid, redolent with virtues, and solemn under the weight of "leaded" articles. And so the editor grows to love his paper. Demanding his constant care, taxing his most patient thought, it becomes the object of his love and the absorbent of his life.

SOCIOLOGY.

We merely chronicle the fact. At Piqua, Ohio, one Thomas Wise courted and said he would marry Mary Macher. He backed out of his promise and engaged himself to another young woman. Last Sunday, with this guilt upon him, he went to the Catholic church; also to the same church went Mary, and took a seat immediately behind Thomas. After she had smoothed out the folds of her dress, she took a horse-pistol out of her muff, placed the muzzle against Thomas' back and fired, blowing a hole through his lungs. Thomas is not expected to recover. "But was there no —?" No, it don't appear that there was anything of that kind at all. Mary seems to have been as chaste as an icicle on the eaves of Diana's woodshed, and Thomas as free from all carnal sin as a graven image.

There is not much to be said about it. It all comes from the law of progress. A woman's right to homicide the man who has been too much allured by her charms has been so frequently affirmed by courts and juries that it may be considered a part of the common law of the country. But to scorn her for the allurements of some hated rival —this is a far greater outrage to sensitive womanhood, and progress demands that it be placed among the capital crimes also. This, at least, seems to have been Miss Mary's view of it when she pursued

Thomas into the sanctuary and slew him at the foot of the altar.

The circle of social ideas and requirements within which a man's life may be considered safe is becoming fearfully narrowed. The Mary Harris case we were not disposed to complain of — for, notwithstanding we thought the alleged offender in that case should have been tried before he was executed, still the moral of the case had no terrors for the young man of "correct habits." But push this Ohio case to its logical results, and where does the man of the period stand? He may enlarge his litany, and cry out, "From raging females and horse pistols in church, Good Lord deliver me!" He may fly to the horns of the altar, and cling to them for safety. In vain — he shall be made to feel that "Hell hath no fury like a woman scorned."

The upshot of it all will be, we suppose, to make social intercourse between ladies and gentlemen impossible. In the present condition of the law of homicide we are not sure but that would be best.